"I've never kissed a ——— before."

A smile played at the corner of her mouth. "I've never kissed a banker before."

"I guess that makes us even." He felt his finger tremble as he traced her moist full lower lip. "I've been waiting a long time to kiss you, Katherine."

He wanted to go slow and easy with her, but he was afraid that once he tasted Katherine, a kiss wouldn't be enough.

She smile bewitchingly. "I only got here yesterday."

He lost the battle before it had even begun. "What in the hell took you so long?" he muttered, before lowering his head and claiming her mouth.

WHAT ARE *LOVESWEPT* ROMANCES?

They are stories of true romance and touching emotion. We believe those two very important ingredients are constants in our highly sensual and very believable stories in the LOVESWEPT line. Our goal is to give you, the reader, stories of consistently high quality that may sometimes make you laugh, sometimes make you cry, but are always fresh and creative and contain many delightful surprises within their pages.

Most romance fans read an enormous number of books. Those they truly love, they keep. Others may be traded with friends and soon forgotten. We hope that each LOVESWEPT romance will be a treasure—a "keeper." We will always try to publish

LOVE STORIES YOU'LL NEVER FORGET BY AUTHORS YOU'LL ALWAYS REMEMBER

The Editors

SILVER IN THE MOONLIGHT

MARCIA EVANICK

BANTAM BOOKS
NEW YORK · TORONTO · LONDON · SYDNEY · AUCKLAND

SILVER IN THE MOONLIGHT
A Bantam Book / October 1998

LOVESWEPT *and the wave design are registered trademarks of Bantam Books, a division of Bantam Doubleday Dell Publishing Group, Inc. Registered in U.S. Patent and Trademark Office and elsewhere.*

All rights reserved.
Copyright © 1998 by Marcia Evanick.
Cover art copyright © 1998 by Barney Plotkin.
No part of this book may be reproduced or transmitted in any form or by any means, electronic or mechanical, including photocopying, recording, or by any information storage and retrieval system, without permission in writing from the publisher.
For information address: Bantam Books.

If you purchased this book without a cover you should be aware that this book is stolen property. It was reported as "unsold and destroyed" to the publisher and neither the author nor the publisher has received any payment for this "stripped book."

ISBN 0-553-44710-6

Published simultaneously in the United States and Canada

Bantam Books are published by Bantam Books, a division of Bantam Doubleday Dell Publishing Group, Inc. Its trademark, consisting of the words "Bantam Books" and the portrayal of a rooster, is Registered in U.S. Patent and Trademark Office and in other countries. Marca Registrada. Bantam Books, 1540 Broadway, New York, New York 10036.

PRINTED IN THE UNITED STATES OF AMERICA
OPM   10 9 8 7 6 5 4 3 2 1

To Delores H.

who showed me that true Southern
hospitality doesn't always
start in the South.

Thanks.

ONE

"Miss Kitty's coming! Miss Kitty's coming!"

Dean Warren Katz glanced over the white picket fence overgrown with monstrous pink rosebushes sprouting two-inch thorns. The fence served as a boundary between his home and the Silver sisters' property. Dean often thought that if Sleeping Beauty's castle had been surrounded by such a prickly barrier, the Prince never would have made it through to give that kiss and have a fairy-tale ending. He smiled at Sadie Silver as she waved a white sheet of paper at him. He stepped closer to the deadly barricade and raised his voice. "What was that, Sadie?" Everyone in town knew doorknobs could hear better than seventy-four-year-old Sadie.

"Miss Kitty's coming!" Sadie wiped her flour-coated hands on the pink gingham-and-lace apron tied around her ample waist.

Marcia Evanick

2

Miss Kitty's coming! Hell, it sounded like the title of a porno flick, or maybe a very risqué rerun of *Gunsmoke*. Sweet senile Sadie might remember the television series, but she probably didn't have the first clue as to what a porno movie was.

"Who's Miss Kitty?" The name sounded familiar and he prayed it wasn't another sister. He didn't think he could handle another Silver sister for a neighbor. Sadie and Ida were more than any sane man or town could cope with.

"She's our niece." Sadie puckered up her wrinkled brow and frowned at the letter clutched in her hand. "No, she's our grandniece, or is it great-niece?" Her frown quickly faded. "She's little Edward's daughter."

Dean had no idea who little Edward was, but the niece part he understood. As far as he knew, the Silver sisters only had one niece. "Oh, you mean Katherine?"

"Of course, Dean. Who did you think I was talking about?" Sadie neatly folded the letter and slipped it into her apron pocket. "Ida's the only one who calls her Katherine. I've been calling her Kitty since she was just a baby. She used to lie in her cradle and make the most adorable little sounds." Sadie took a couple steps toward the thorny hedge and beamed with pride. "She was such a playful child, just like a little kitten. Always getting into mischief and always wanting to be cuddled."

Kitty Silver! Lord save Jasper, South Carolina,

Silver in the Moonlight

3

Dean thought. Another Silver was coming. Kitty Silver sounded like the headliner for a strip joint that specialized in watered-down drinks and lap dances. And it was all his fault. He was the one who had written to Katherine Silver, who lived in Boston, and informed her of her great-aunts' deteriorating mental faculties.

There was a saying that went, "just a few bricks shy of a full load." Well, in the case of Ida and Sadie Silver, they were lucky to still be possessing enough bricks between them to fill a four-year-old's little red wagon. He had written to Katherine Silver because she was the only family Ida and Sadie ever mentioned, and he hoped she would "see the light" and help the concerned citizens of Jasper relocate her great-aunts into a peaceful and well-run rest home on the outskirts of town.

"Does she say when she's coming?" he asked. He tried to appear polite, not overly eager.

"Of course she does, Dean." Sadie shook her head at what she obviously considered an absurd question. "I've got to run, I've got a gooseberry pie in the oven." Sadie turned hurriedly toward the house, then stopped and muttered, "Oh dear, Kitty hates gooseberry pie."

Dean watched as Sadie bustled back into the house. She hadn't answered his question. Nothing unusual there. Sadie never really answered questions. Sadie baked. All day, every day, Sadie baked enough pies, cakes, turnovers, buns, muffins, and breads to feed half the population of Jasper. He was one of the many recipients of her delicious talent and work. Every other day, like clockwork, one of the Silver sisters stood at his door and welcomed him to the neighborhood with a home-baked goodie. He had been living next door to them for eighteen months now. Thanks to the Silver sisters he had taken up jogging and laid out a nice chunk of cash for the exercise equipment filling one of the bedrooms in his house.

At least one of his problems was about to be solved. Miss Kitty was coming. Maybe now he would get the Revitalization of Jasper Committee off his back. The Silver sisters' Greek Revival home had been built before the Civil War and could be one of Jasper's sparkling jewels. Instead, it was in the process of falling down upon the Silver sisters' heads. Sadie was always busy at the oven and Ida was forever down on her knees in the gardens. Neither had an inclination to look up once in a while to see what was on its way down.

Dean shook his head, taking in again the faded paint, the broken shutters, the overgrown gardens. More times than he could count he had been over there pounding nails into their steps or tacking down a loose board on the veranda. He wasn't a carpenter by trade, but since they saw no need to call one, he had done the neighborly thing. The last thing he wanted was for Sadie or Ida to trip over a loose board and break a hip or

Silver in the Moonlight

something. Their house was becoming a hazard, and it was about time someone in their family learned the sad truth. Sadie and Ida were no longer capable of living on their own.

He shook his head over the situation, but there was nothing more he could do. He wasn't even entirely comfortable with what he had done. He had copied Katherine Silver's address from one of her letters that had been lying on a mahogany table by the front door and, without telling Sadie and Ida, had written to her. If Sadie and Ida had received Katherine's letter in today's mail, it probably would be a couple more weeks before he'd see their precious niece.

He picked up his own mail and headed up onto his porch. A letter from his sister caught his attention. Amanda's letters always brightened his day. He opened the envelope before he even unlocked his front door. He got as far as the salutation when the roar of a powerful engine shattered the peace of the quiet neighborhood. He curiously lowered his sister's letter and watched as a red vintage MGB whipped up the Silver's driveway and came to an abrupt stop.

The gleam of the setting sun bounced off the red sports car, half blinding him and rousing a twinge of envy. The little two-seater was a beauty, but it was the woman climbing out of it who captured and held his attention. From the shadows of his porch he was too far away to get a close look, but he still saw plenty.

Luscious blonde hair was pulled up into a high ponytail, and was definitely windblown from driving with the rag top down. Dark sunglasses hid her eyes, but her mouth appeared to be smiling. She was wearing a white polo shirt and a pair of jeans that clung to every curve like a fine glove, and dazzling white sneakers. Whoever she was, one word popped foremost into his mind; cute. He would have added wholesome to that description except for the car. Cute, wholesome women didn't drive red sports cars, and they didn't drive them like a bat out of hell.

His mouth went dry and he nearly lost his grip on the mail as she reached both hands up over her head and worked the kinks out of her back. Plump breasts stretched the white shirt tight across her chest. Desire rushed to his gut as she then stretched from side to side, giving him a cardiac workout while he stood completely still on his porch.

Over the course of his thirty-four years of life he had had plenty of opportunities to be in the company of beautiful women. But he had never seen a woman move with such simple flowing grace. The evening sun gleamed off a bracelet on her slim right arm. The golden ponytail provocatively brushed the back of her neck with each gentle sway.

He barely held back a deep groan as she bent over and placed her hands on the crushed-shell driveway. A nicely rounded denim-covered bottom bounced in the air. It was the most enticing view he had ever had in his life. It seemed like she was performing for his personal entertainment, yet he doubted if she even knew she had an audience. The temptation pounding through his gut was nearly painful.

Little Miss Hot Rod's arrival had stirred up more than a few crushed shells.

He watched as she straightened and leaned over the closed car door, snatching up a small purse before heading for the house. He lost her in the shadows of the porch, but he could hear her knock. A moment later the screeching of the screen door reached his ears along with Sadie's startled cry of "Kitty!" Ida's cry of "Katherine!" echoed across the yard, followed by the slamming of the screen door.

He stood there for a long moment contemplating the Silver sisters' home and their guest. Miss Kitty was not only coming, she had arrived.

Katherine Rochelle Silver closed her eyes and allowed the night sounds and scents to wash over her. The tension headache that had been building for days was about to erupt into one massive blowup, and every ounce of fallout could be directed at one person, Dean Warren Katz. How dare that man scare ten years off her life! When she received his letter more than a week earlier, panic had seized her heart. She had immediately called her aunts and they seemed fine, but even after hearing their voices, doubts had remained. The way this Katz guy described Sadie and Ida she had been expecting them to be wearing their underwear on their heads, planting magical beans, and wandering the streets of Jasper in dazed confusion.

Instead they had greeted her with open arms, a readied room, and gooseberry pie. The sweet dears were inside cleaning up the kitchen and fussing about what to cook for tomorrow. They had insisted she take a stroll in the back gardens. She didn't want to upset them, so she left them to their puttering.

It had taken her a week to get her things in order, take a temporary leave from her job, and drive south. One very long, nerve-racking week. It was all for nothing. Sadie and Ida seemed perfectly sane and just as sweet as she remembered them. So what if they were a little forgetful! They were both in their seventies. She sure as hell hoped she was half as alert and independent when she reached their age.

Katherine glanced behind her at the house that had been in her family for generations. The house she couldn't remember from her youth, but did remember from more recent visits. This was her fourth visit to her aunts. The last time had been a year earlier, in the spring. They had been extremely disappointed that their neighbor Dean Katz had been away on business at the

Silver in the Moonlight

time. They had so wanted her to meet the nice banker from next door.

Her aunts didn't have to worry about their making each other's acquaintance during this visit. She could guarantee she would be meeting Dean Katz. She would also be leaving him a piece of her mind, roughly the size of Massachusetts.

She frowned at the silhouette of her aunts' house against the starlit sky. Even to her untrained eye, the roof appeared to be sagging. Lights burned warmly at many of the windows, but still the house had a look of sadness—or was it just age? The gardens that Ida so lovingly attended looked oppressive and overgrown instead of gracious and genteel. The fragrance of flowering blooms was more cloying than alluring. The gathering darkness and still evening air only made it all appear and smell worse.

Beyond the back garden was a rolling lawn that ended at the river's edge. The uncluttered lawn and gently flowing water drew her forward. She needed space and air to breathe and think. What was she going to do about her aunts?

Technically they weren't her aunts, they were her great-aunts. They were her father's aunts, but Edward Hamilton Silver had washed his hands of his family years ago. She was the only family Ida and Sadie had left who still took an interest in them. Even her younger brother, Roland, honored their father's wish that they ignore their Southern roots. She couldn't, or as her father claimed, wouldn't. Both of her parents would swear on a stack of Bibles twelve feet tall that their daughter purposely did the exact opposite of whatever she was told.

She would be the first to admit that generally her parents' claim was true, but not in this case. There was something about the South that pulled at her heart. Even though she lived deep in Yankee country, Boston, she felt the pull of the South and the love of her aunts.

If Sadie and Ida were indeed incapable of making a decision, as nosy Mr. Katz seemed to think, then she would be the one calling the shots. Not some uppity banker, or the other concerned citizens of Jasper, and surely not the well-staffed, bingo-playing, green-Jell-O-eating rest home on the outskirts of town. River View Rest Home, ha! Her aunts already had a river view, right in their own backyard.

Katherine walked to the river's edge and frowned at the dark glistening water. The light from the full moon bounced off the shimmering surface. Now that she was there, she didn't know where to start or what to do. How did one determine if two sweet old ladies were still operating on all six cylinders instead of just one or two? Look in the basement to see if they were burying yellow-fever victims or serving elderberry wine to lonely old men?

"Did you know that moonlight turns your hair to silver?"

Silver in the Moonlight

11

She quickly turned in the direction of the deep Southern voice, nearly tripping over her own two feet. "Jiminy Cricket!" She pressed her hand over her pounding heart. She had to remember she was in Jasper, South Carolina, not Boston. "Don't sneak up on a person like that." It was a real shame her Mace was in her purse back at the house or she would have been tempted to give him a big-city squirt and teach him a lesson.

"I didn't mean to startle you." The man took a hesitant step closer. "I thought you might have seen me." His arm motioned to the yard beside her aunts'. "I was standing there when you came out. I didn't want you to get the impression we aren't neighborly down here in Jasper."

Her eyes narrowed as she gazed at the man cloaked in darkness, the yard behind him, and the house next to her aunts'. There was only one person he could be, the pompous Dean Katz, Mr. Stuffy Banker himself. His silhouette didn't look pompous. She wished the moon would come back out from behind that cloud so she could get a better look at him. "Neighborly? You call writing me a letter informing me my aunts are senile and need to be put in a rest home neighborly?"

"I see introductions won't be necessary." He held out his hand. "You must be Katherine Silver or, as Sadie likes to call you, Kitty."

Katherine glared at his hand, not reaching out to shake it. "The name's Katherine or Miss Silver. Never, and I repeat, never, Kitty."

Dean chuckled softly. "Better shake my hand. If I know Sadie and Ida, they're peering out from behind their faded lace curtains spying on us." His hand reached farther. "It would upset them greatly if their favorite niece didn't get along with their neighbor."

She knew he had a point there, but it didn't mean she had to like it. She reached for his hand and gave it a quick shake. "I'm their only niece, Mr. Katz." His hand was warm and firm within her grasp. It didn't feel like the hand of some banker who shuffled money all day.

"That automatically makes you their favorite."

She dropped his hand. Between the warm tingly sensation spreading up her arm and the rich smoothness of his deep voice, she was beginning to get a strange feeling about her aunts' neighbor. His Southern drawl was barely noticeable and was sexy as hell. The darkness prevented her from seeing his features clearly, but she understood one thing. She had sadly misjudged Dean Warren Katz. He definitely wasn't some middle-aged, potbellied, pretentious banker. "My aunts speak very highly of you, Mr. Katz."

"My friends call me Dean."

"I take it Ida and Sadie haven't the foggiest idea that you want someone to sell their home out from under them and shove them into a rest home, *Mr. Katz*?"

She watched as he rubbed the back of his

Silver in the Moonlight

13

neck. The pale light from the moon, which finally came out from behind that cloud, lit his features enough so she could get a good look at him. Her heart climbed up her throat, only to plummet to her knees. Dean Katz was one of the most handsome men she'd ever seen. His face matched his voice, which matched the warmth of his touch, which in turn matched every fantasy she'd ever had about a man.

"I have a feeling you took my letter the wrong way."

"I didn't think there was another way to take it, Mr. Katz." What did it matter what he looked like? she asked herself. He was still the person who'd written the letter and caused her unbelievable stress.

"I think this might be a case of wanting to kill the messenger." Dean sighed. "Listen, Katherine, I'm sorry I had to be the one to write to you, but someone had to."

"You hinted that their playing deck was missing quite a few cards and you explicitly stated that the house was falling down around their ears." She took a deep breath and vented her frustration. "I rush down here, only to find them as sane and sweet as last year. Granted their minds might not be as sharp as tacks, but I'll wager they could still puncture a few balloons. The house is still standing, and except for the little sag in the roof, it appears to be in good shape."

"That little sag, as you so naively put it, is a

sign of a larger, more serious problem. Tomorrow, take some time and wander around both the inside and outside of the house. One hint—Sadie and Ida have become experts at moving furniture, pictures, and such to hide or cover problems. I'm not expecting you to take my word for it, Katherine. I'm a banker, not a contractor. Call someone and have them come out and inspect the house. Just make sure they inspect the foundation. My gut is telling me it's crumbling, which *is* going to bring the entire house down on their white-haired heads."

"You're trying to scare me, aren't you?"

"No, I'm trying to make someone do something. I've been after Sadie and Ida for nearly a year now to get someone to come out and inspect the place. But they won't listen to me. They keep telling me that Hamilton took real good care of the place and it could withstand another war if the South decides to once again secede from the Union."

Katherine couldn't prevent the chuckle that escaped her throat. Sadie and Ida hadn't been alive during the Civil War, but they had been raised on the stories. Every Southern belle worth her petticoats and hoop skirts believed the South would rise again. "My grandfather, Hamilton Silver, died three years ago."

"I know, and no one has touched the house since. Your grandfather was eighty-three when he died, Katherine. I really don't think he was doing any major construction work around here, do you?"

She frowned at her aunts' house. In one of the upstairs bedrooms a curtain moved. Dean had been right, they were being spied upon. "Nothing's been done to the house in three years?" Why hadn't she given any thought to how her aunts were managing the upkeep on such a large house all these years? They always seemed so lively and cheerful when she called them, she just assumed they were getting along fine.

"I've tacked down a few loose boards and a step or two, but nothing major. I wouldn't know where to begin."

"You? You've been helping my aunts?"

"I told you, Katherine, Jasper is a nice friendly little town where neighbors help each other all the time. Sadie and Ida's problems have gotten bigger than this neighbor can handle, so I took it upon myself to write to their niece for some help."

"So what you are telling me is that I've misread the situation. You don't want to toss them into some rest home? You aren't the one who mentioned River View Rest Home in your letter to me?" Now she was totally confused. The man fixed her aunts' steps out of the kindness of his heart, yet claimed they belonged behind the well-supervised gates of River View.

"I only mentioned River View because I didn't know if you cared one way or another what happened to your aunts. You live hundreds of miles away and I would have to assume you do have a life in Boston. As far as I knew, it might not be convenient for you to handle Sadie and Ida's problems."

"Convenient!" she sputtered in outrage. "How dare you say it isn't convenient for me to care about my aunts."

He shrugged. "Listen, I know you were down here last year at this time. I'm sorry we didn't meet then. Maybe we would have had a chance to get to know each other and then I wouldn't have assumed Sadie and Ida's deteriorating mental, as well as physical, abilities would be an inconvenience for you."

Now she was really ticked. How dare he assume she didn't care about her aunts. "I happen to call my aunts at least every other week and we correspond weekly. I've never once suspected that they were slipping mentally. And if you're referring to Ida's heart condition, I know all about it. I've even talked to her cardiologist in Beaufont on several occasions."

"Do you know about the fire that damaged their dining room New Year's Eve? Sadie forgot to blow out the candles they had lit before she went to bed."

"I—"

"What about the time Ida wandered away from the house? It took half the town all day to find her. She was out in Hangman Swamp looking for buried treasure."

"Hangman Swamp!" Lord, wasn't that the place where alligators ruled and the occasional black bear still roamed? What in the world had Ida been doing out there?

"I could go on, Katherine."

"Don't, please." She didn't think she could handle knowing what else her aunts had been up to while she was busy getting on with her boring life in Boston. Both of her aunts could have been killed by the fire, or Ida could have become some alligator's lunch. How could two sweet old ladies have pulled the wool over her eyes for all this time?

Well, it was time to push the wool away. She was their niece and it was her responsibility to see that they were safe and happy. Dean Katz was right, Sadie and Ida weren't his responsibility, or the town's. He had done the right thing by informing her of the situation. How she was going to handle it was a different matter. First she had to figure how bad the situation really was, then she could work on a solution. One that didn't entail River View Rest Home.

"I think I owe you an apology, Mr. Katz."

"I told you the name is Dean, and your apology is accepted." Dean's smile was pure magic. She felt it melt her kneecaps and curl her toes within her sneakers. "Your anger at me for insinuating your aunts aren't operating with a full deck was warranted, and it showed me that you really do care for them. I've grown very fond of Ida and Sadie myself during the past eighteen months. I'm glad they have you now to help them make whatever decisions need to be made."

Katherine decided she didn't like his smile one bit. If it held that much power in the moonlight, she shuddered to think what it would be like if it were directed solely at her in broad daylight. "I'm not sure how much help I'm going to be. This whole aging process has me puzzled. Shouldn't they be sitting in rocking chairs and knitting or something?"

Dean chuckled. "I've never seen either one of your aunts knit. Last week I was called upon to help Sadie thread a needle because neither one of them could see well enough to find the eye." His hand was warm and gentle as he cupped her elbow and started to walk her back up the lawn toward her aunts' house. "My advice is to take your time and get to know them better. The problems will become apparent, but hopefully, with some time, so will the solutions."

She let him walk her through the overgrown garden that had spilled into the pathways. He seemed so calm and sure that she would be able to do whatever her aunts needed. She wished she had half his confidence. Now that she had gotten a better picture of what was happening, her anger had shifted its focus. She was now furious with herself for not realizing sooner that her

Silver in the Moonlight

aunts needed her. Dean Katz was a wonderful neighbor and a dear friend of her aunts. He shouldn't have had to write her and apprise her of the situation.

The curtain in the upstairs window fluttered again, catching her attention. "You were right, my aunts are peering out from behind their lace curtains."

Dean stopped by the steps leading up to the small back porch. They were now out of sight of the upstairs window. "It was only Sadie." He dropped his hand away from her arm.

"How do you know?"

"Because if it had been Ida, she would have been at the back door by now giving me a lecture on taking liberties with her niece."

"Liberties? What liberties?" There was no way a gorgeous man could have taken liberties without her being aware of it. She knew there was a different code of etiquette in the South, but really! Someone should be standing at the Mason-Dixon Line handing out literature to incoming visitors. A woman had the right to know when liberties were being taken so she could appreciate them better.

"I was holding your arm as we walked back to the house," Dean explained. "Ida has a very strict code of behavior when it comes to men." His smile was friendly and warm. "I believe arm holding comes after the engagement has been announced and hand-holding is never done in public."

Arm holding! she thought. Since when had arm holding become a liberty? "Oh, I'll keep that in mind." She really didn't care about Ida's strict code of behavior or what the South considered liberties. She wasn't planning on being involved with any man while she was there, no matter what he looked like in the moonlight. "I want to thank you, Dean."

"You must have forgiven me, Katherine. You called me Dean."

"Of course I've forgiven you for scaring ten years off my life. I needed the scare. What I want to thank you for is being a good friend and neighbor to my aunts." She reached up and kissed his cheek. Liberties be damned. "Not many people would have befriended a pair of old ladies just because they lived next door."

His fingers touched the spot her lips had just kissed. "You can thank me like that anytime you want."

She laughed softly. That would be the day, when a man who looked like Dean got all excited about a simple thank-you peck on the cheek. She didn't care what the Southern etiquette book had to say on the subject, men who looked like Dean had a lot of experience with a woman's touch. "Do you want to come in? I'm sure Sadie has some of that gooseberry pie left."

He groaned and took a hasty step back. "As

much as I would love the company, I better not. I'm up to jogging two miles every morning, and if I eat any more of your aunt's baking it will soon be three."

As she allowed her gaze to slide down his body, her opinion of jogging reached an all-time high. She'd been bombarded and tempted with Sadie's baking enough in the past and she knew exactly what Dean was referring to. Last spring she had gained seven pounds during a five-day visit. "I better be going in, then." She started up the steps to the porch. "I'm sure we'll be seeing each other around."

Glancing back at him before she walked into the house, she saw Dean give her a funny look that she couldn't interpret. "Count on it, Katherine," he said.

TWO

Katherine slowly pulled back the fragile lace curtain hanging over her bedroom window and studied the view of Jackson Avenue. The sun had just won its daily battle with the night. Pale morning sunlight, a cool breeze, and the singing of a chorus of birds rushed in through the screen and greeted her. A young boy on a red bicycle zigzagged his way up the street tossing newspapers onto dew-kissed yards and occasionally a well-aimed-for porch.

Morning had broken, and with it came the sad knowledge that she wouldn't be seeing her aunts in the same light as she had in the past. Starting that day she had to scrutinize everything they said or did. She had to evaluate her great-aunts and possibly decide their future.

It was a sobering thought.

She couldn't even figure out what to do with

her own future, let alone two elderly aunts she barely knew. She had been only four years old when her family moved from Charleston to Boston. Any memory of Sadie and Ida from those early years had been obliterated with time. As she grew, her only contact with her aunts had been the much-anticipated birthday and Christmas presents that arrived bearing fat bows and the fragrant scent of jasmine. Every year two more porcelain dolls were added to what had become a very impressive collection. It wasn't until she graduated from college and started working for a travel agency that she had had a chance to visit them.

During the quick and not-so-quick trips she had grown to love the sweet old ladies. But did she really know them? She had listened to their childhood memories, heard stories of her grandfather Silver, and felt their love. But did she really know them well enough to decide their future?

Did anyone ever know another person well enough to decide their future?

It was a heavy question. One that had kept her tossing and turning far into the night. One that had been playing across her mind and had pulled her from sleep long before the dawn claimed the sky.

The banging of a wooden screen door pulled her attention from troubling thoughts. From the upstairs bedroom window she had a bird's-eye view of Dean Katz's house and she had to wonder why the banker was up so early. As he stepped off his porch she had her answer. Dean Katz was about to go jogging. Either that or he was out to drive the female population of Jasper into cardiac arrest.

Her aunts' neighbor had the most gorgeous legs she had ever seen on a man. They were long, tanned, and finely muscled. The skimpy red running shorts he wore showed them off to perfection. The white T-shirt, clinging to his chest, had red letters on the front, but she couldn't make out the words. Low white socks and a dirty pair of white sneakers completed his meager, and incredibly sexy, attire.

She hadn't been attracted to jocks during her college years. Men who used their brains always impressed her more than those with bulging biceps and buns of steel. She frowned as Dean stretched out the muscles in his legs. Maybe she had wasted four good years. Then again, she couldn't remember any of the boys at Amherst College looking like Dean.

In the bright light of the morning she could see that she had misjudged how attractive Dean really was. Last night she had thought he was handsome. This morning she leaned toward heart-stoppingly gorgeous.

She barely breathed as he finished his warm-up and took off down the street at an easy run. She pressed her nose against the screen, trying to get a better look, as he rounded the bend in the

Silver in the Moonlight

street and disappeared from view. If she hadn't been awake before Dean's appearance, she was now. Fully awake. She didn't have to worry about Sadie serving only decaf coffee with breakfast. Her body had had its morning jolt, and it didn't contain one ounce of caffeine. The American Heart Association would have approved.

The delicious aroma of baking cinnamon bread pulled her from the window and sent her heading for the shower.

Twenty minutes later she entered the kitchen and came to an abrupt halt. Sadie was in the middle of icing a platterful of cinnamon rolls and Ida was standing at the sink arranging freshly cut flowers in a vase. Both activities were harmless in themselves and hadn't caused her sudden apprehension. The amount of baked goods and overflowing vases cluttering the table and counter did.

"Good morning, Sadie." She brushed a kiss over her aunt's cheek and then went to stand next to Ida. "'Morning, Ida." She took the vase of roses and placed a kiss on Ida's crinkled cheek. "You two are up early this morning."

Ida smiled. "There's so much to do we couldn't sleep."

"You're just in time," Sadie said as she iced the last bun and placed it back on the platter.

"For what?" She frowned at the two dozen cupcakes, three loaves of what appeared to be banana-nut bread, the cinnamon buns, and a large bowl filled with chocolate-chip-cookie batter.

Her aunts had to have awakened hours ago. "You need my help hauling all this to the bake sale?"

"Goodness no," Sadie said as the timer on the oven went off. She hurried over to the oven, pulled two sheets of cookies from it, and inserted the next two sheets without missing a beat. "The church bake sale was last week."

"Then who is all this for?" Katherine placed the vase of roses next to one containing irises and waved her hand at the table filled with at least a million, possibly a trillion, calories.

"Why, it's for you, Kitty!" Sadie beamed as she plucked a freshly iced bun off the platter and placed it on a plate, then handed it to her. "Last time you were here you said how much you enjoyed my baking."

Katherine looked at the table with a dawning sense of horror. Her aunts were going to force-feed her goodies until she exploded. "Do you mean to tell me all of this is for me?" She suddenly didn't feel like biting into the cinnamon bun Sadie had handed her, and set the plate back onto the table.

"Oh my, not all of it, Kitty." Sadie chuckled as she took down a plate and started arranging warm chocolate-chip cookies on it. "We need you to take this over to Dean for us." Sadie covered the plate with a rose-colored linen napkin and handed it to her. "You met him last night during your little stroll."

"I know who Dean is. I even know where he

Silver in the Moonlight

lives. What I don't know is why you want me to take cookies to him at this hour in the morning." It was barely after seven, and as far as she knew, the man was still out jogging off an earlier batch of warm gooey chocolate-chip cookies.

In a strange way she had to feel sorry for Dean, being her aunts' neighbor and the object of their kindness. Proper manners, along with a good dose of guilt, would force him to try everything Sadie sent over to him. She would rather go bald and have all her teeth fall out than start every morning by jogging two miles.

"The dear boy loves my chocolate-chip cookies still warm from the oven."

Katherine suppressed a groan. Calling Dean a *dear boy* was like referring to a peregrine falcon as a sweet birdy. "Do you always bring him cookies this early in the morning?" She glanced out the kitchen window toward Dean's house. Maybe if she hurried she could get an up-close-and-personal glimpse of those incredible legs. She could think of worse ways to start her day. Like jogging.

"Now that the days are turning warmer I try to get all my baking done in the morning while it's still cool." Sadie hustled her toward the door. "You better hurry. Dean doesn't like to be late for work."

Katherine shook her head with amazement as a moment later she stood on the side veranda holding a plate of warm cookies and facing

Dean's house. She wasn't positive, but Sadie had seemed quite pleased with herself. Ida had stood quietly in the corner jamming tall spiky purple flowers into a crystal vase. Whatever was pleasing Sadie seemed to be upsetting Ida. As she walked toward Dean's house along the uneven slate path, which was overrun with grass and weeds, she had to wonder if it had anything to do with her or the early-morning mission Sadie had just sent her on.

She squeezed through an opening where a gate had once hung, but that was now guarded by pink rosebushes. Thorny pink rosebushes, as the thin, bleeding scratch on her thigh would testify to. She muttered a very unladylike curse and promised to revisit the deadly barrier with a pair of sharp hedge clippers.

A minute later she was knocking on the wooden screen door at the back of Dean's house. The aroma of freshly brewed coffee tantalized her senses. She had to wonder what the chances were of Dean being a decaf drinker and how it would look if she held his cookies for ransom.

Dean opened the screen door. "Good morning, Katherine." His welcoming smile faded as he spied the napkin-covered plate in her hand. "Please tell me that's not what I think it is." His voice held a hint of desperation and a touch of laughter all rolled up into that sexy Southern accent.

She grinned and waved the plate under his nose as she walked by him. "Sadie says you can't resist her chocolate-chip cookies still warm from the oven." The view from her window earlier hadn't fully prepared her for the devastating effect of being less than twelve inches away from Dean in broad daylight. The man radiated sex appeal like the sun radiated heat. Both could scorch her on the spot.

Dean's nose seemed to follow the plate. "Pay the woman a compliment once and she'll never forget it."

Katherine eyed his coffeemaker with renewed hope. The deep dark brew filled the glass pot to the brim. There was more than enough for two. "Oh, so you really don't want these?"

Dean allowed the screen door to close. "I didn't say that." He took a step closer to the plate she was holding and sniffed.

She was disappointed that he was no longer dressed in his running outfit, but the white dress shirt, brown pants, and conservative striped tie draped untied over his shoulders were devastating in their own right. His hair was still damp from his shower and his face had that "just shaved" look. She could smell his aftershave. It held the hint of windswept beaches and luxury yachts. She knew that scent; it was the smell of money.

The top two buttons on his shirt were still undone and gave her a tempting view of his deeply tanned throat and a hint of what appeared to be one scrumptious-looking chest. A swirl of dark hair peeked out, tempting her fingers to release the next button or so just to see what else he might be hiding behind his civil facade.

The banker's clothes, she decided, were just as seductive as the skimpy red running shorts, maybe more so. His jogging outfit left very little to the imagination, while the businessman's attire offered a lot, and all of it tempting. She forced her gaze away from him and back to the coffeepot. Dean Katz was her aunts' neighbor. A seemingly nice and concerned neighbor, but a neighbor nonetheless. She was in Jasper to help her aunts and to think about her own future, not drool on the local banker's chest.

She held the plate out of his reach and couldn't resist teasing. "Delivery service is going to cost you."

His gaze jerked from the plate to her face, and the look that leaped into his eyes had nothing to do with the cookies or even food. But it had everything to do with hunger. Adult hunger. "I'm willing to pay."

The low husky timbre of his voice sent shock waves rippling through her stomach. His gaze scorched her mouth and she had to swallow a low groan as her body instinctively responded to his look. She would have to have been at least ninety-five years old not to have responded. Then again, even being ninety-five might not have prevented the desire that was streaking through her body.

Dean had reacted to her playful teasing with a seriousness that threw her off balance. She hadn't

Silver in the Moonlight

been prepared for the flash of desire that darkened his brown eyes to nearly black. She also hadn't been prepared for her own body's response. She wanted whatever Dean's heated gaze was promising.

She was twenty-nine years old and knew that just wanting something didn't mean it would be good for her. Giving in to this yearning for Dean Katz might be good for her body, but not for her soul. She pulled her gaze away from him and glanced at his coffeepot. "The going price for home delivery is a cup of coffee." She handed him the plate and offered him a smile. A nice neighborly smile. "As long as it isn't decaf."

"A cup of coffee, is that the current rate?" He placed the plate of cookies on the counter and pulled two cups out of the cabinet. "I was willing to go much higher."

She refused to look at him to see if the heat was still in his eyes. From the low tone of his voice, she would have to guess that it was. She watched as he filled a cup and handed it to her. "I cut you a break because you've been awfully nice to my aunts." She concentrated on the aroma drifting from the cup and took a deep breath.

"It's part of my Southern charm. Grandpappy would be awfully disappointed in me if I failed to lend a helping hand to two lone females. Especially two as fine as Sadie and Ida. True Southern belles are becoming an endangered species around these parts." He filled his own cup and replaced the pot. "What do you take in it?"

"Nothing, I drink it black." She raised the cup. "Thanks. I've been called completely uncivil in the morning if I don't get my caffeine quota."

Dean leaned against the counter and sipped his own coffee. He would love to see Katherine "completely uncivil" in the morning. Preferably while she was naked, in his bed, and under him.

He choked on his coffee as it went down the wrong pipe. Where in the hell had that come from? He knew where, his dream from last night. It was one thing to have erotic dreams about Sadie and Ida's precious niece. It was completely another to be fantasizing about her over coffee in his kitchen. Especially while she was standing less than two feet away from him.

Katherine pounded him on the back while he tried to regain his breath without appearing too much like an idiot. He held up a hand to ward off her next blow and managed to choke out, "I'm fine."

"Really?"

He rapidly blinked the moisture out of his eyes and studied her face. She didn't look too convinced of that fact. "I'm fine, Katherine." He felt like a clumsy moron but knew of no graceful way out of the situation. "Sorry about that, but I appreciate your coming to my rescue." It hadn't felt like a rescue to him. It had felt like she was trying to pound a few of his vertebrae out through his chest. "I was having a hard time trying to picture you being uncivil."

"Uncivil is my mother's way of saying I'm unfit for human contact before my morning jolt of caffeine. My brother more accurately calls me a grouch." She uncovered the cookies and offered him one. "Maybe a cookie will help."

He reached for a cookie even though he wasn't sure his throat was up to working properly. "Help me what? Think of you as a grouch?" He took a sip of coffee and was relieved when everything went down the right pipes. He relaxed and bite into the warm cookie. Sadie was right. He couldn't resist her chocolate-chip cookies straight from the oven. Heck, he couldn't resist them three days old and sitting in his cookie jar.

"Take my mother's and brother's word for it, I'm an uncivil grouch without my coffee and all Sadie and Ida brew is decaf." Katherine reached for a cookie and took a big bite.

He watched as she polished off the cookie and couldn't imagine her as a grouch. He wondered if there had been, or still was, anyone else in her life who had intimate knowledge of her morning outlook. His glance shot to her left hand and the two rings she was wearing. One was a ruby pinkie ring and the other was a nice-sized amethyst, but it was on the wrong finger. Or the right finger, depending on how you looked at it. He took the lack of ring on her third finger as a good sign.

Lord, she was gorgeous. Even dressed in casual navy shorts, sandals, and a red-white-and-navy-striped top, she was stunning enough to stir his blood. She had left her hair down so that it brushed her shoulders in blonde waves and made his fingers itch to touch its softness. Stress and a restless night were in evidence in the lines around her mouth and the circles under her eyes, but the eyes themselves were clear and bright. For the first time he noticed that her eyes held a hint of mischief. It was almost as if the spark of devilment was there naturally, as if she had been born with it.

He contemplated that spark as he sipped more coffee and allowed his gaze to travel down her body. He nearly choked on the hot liquid again as he spotted the long scratch on the outside of her thigh. "You're bleeding!"

She glanced down at her leg and shrugged. "It's only a scratch," she said, reaching for another cookie. "Something has to be done with those rosebushes. They're lethal."

"You need to put something on it." He set his cup on the counter and strode to the downstairs bathroom, where he kept antiseptic and bandages, ignoring Katherine's protest as he rummaged through the medicine cabinet. The sight of her blood had sent a wave of childhood fears crashing through his body.

When he was six years old he had cut his arm on a tree he shouldn't have been climbing. The nanny his parents had hired saw the cut and im-

Silver in the Moonlight

mediately feared for her job. She decided to scare him into never climbing a tree again by relating all kinds of terrible things that could develop from a simple cut. The descriptions had run from seeping infections to gangrene to amputations. For weeks he'd had nightmares of doctors amputating his arm. The nanny had been dismissed, but the damage had been done. Fear of injuring himself had turned him into the biggest sissy in his school.

Over the years he had learned to hide, if not control, his fear, but he never took any chance when it came to fighting an infection. Katherine's leg needed immediate medical treatment. He gathered his supplies and hurried back to the kitchen.

She looked at the assortment of tubes, creams, and sprays as he placed them on the counter, and chuckled. "It's only a little scratch, Dean, not a gaping wound."

"It can still get infected." He frowned at the beaded line of blood. It didn't look too bad, but one could never tell with an open wound. "You need to put some antiseptic on it."

"I'll wash when I get back to my aunts'."

He picked up the white washcloth he had brought from the bathroom and ran it under warm water. "Here, use this."

She eyed him curiously for a moment before taking the washcloth from his hand. "Playing doctor is going to cost you."

He glanced at her empty coffee cup and grinned. "Help yourself." Katherine seemed to be willing to do a lot of things for coffee. He had to remember that for the future.

She poured herself another cup, braced her foot on a chair, and carefully pressed the cloth onto the cut.

Dean watched her closely for any signs of pain, but all he could detect was her blissful pleasure in drinking coffee. He ignored the lush sight of her lightly tanned thigh and the provocative curve of the rest of her leg as he lifted the cloth. The scrape was about six inches in length, but didn't appear too deep. It had already stopped bleeding.

"Well, doc, do you think I'll live?"

"If you're lucky it won't even scar." He turned to the counter and selected a green-and-white bottle of first-aid spray that was guaranteed to kill germs on contact. He uncapped the top and sprayed a generous amount directly onto the cut. Katherine's sudden intake of breath startled him. "Did that hurt?" The spray pledged not to sting or burn. Maybe the cut wasn't as innocent as it appeared.

"No, you didn't hurt me, but that spray was ice-cold."

He mustered a small smile and quickly dabbed at the clear liquid that had missed the cut before she noticed how his fingers trembled. "Sorry about that." Her thigh felt warm and soft

Silver in the Moonlight

beneath his touch. He stepped back and handed her a tube of antiseptic cream. "The cut is too long for a bandage. Put this on it to help protect it."

She glanced at the tube. "Are you sure all this is necessary? All I did was rub up against Ida's treacherous rosebushes."

He needed to lighten the situation before Katherine thought he was some deranged paranoid with a fixation on thighs or blood. "You never know where that thorn has been." He turned to rinse out the washcloth because he didn't want to watch her spread on the medicated cream. "Speaking of thorns, what do you think the chances are that you could convince Ida to do some pruning on those rosebushes?"

"I'll make it my first priority if you make an extra cup of coffee in the morning every once in a while."

He had to smile at the hopeful look on her face. Being an avid coffee drinker himself, he understood the yearning for that first cup in the morning. "Consider my door open and my coffeepot filled for as long as you need it." He topped off her cup and poured the rest of the pot into his. He could always grab another cup or two at work. "Put the scalping of the rosebushes farther down on your list. I think you should concentrate more on your aunts first."

"That's the problem, Dean." Katherine took

a sip of coffee before glancing at him. "I don't know where to begin."

"Talk to them, Katherine. Ask them if they're having any problems or difficulties managing. If they aren't forthcoming, which would be my guess, ask them about the future. Ask them what they want."

"What if what they want isn't possible?"

"Then you have some hard decisions to make. Sadie and Ida are both very strong and independent-minded females. They will fight you if they don't like your decisions." Katherine didn't look strong enough to weather a verbal battle against the aunts she loved. Then again, last night she had stood her ground when she thought he had been out to harm her aunts. In this case, he hoped looks were deceiving. "What about your father, little Edward? Can't he come down and give you a hand? He *is* their only nephew."

Katherine chuckled. "Only Sadie and Ida would have the guts to call my father "little Edward" and no, he won't come. He claims the family disowned him twenty-five years ago, while Sadie and Ida both claim he disowned his family." She shrugged. "The story has been distorted with time, but take my word for it, my father won't be coming to Jasper."

"So it's all going to fall on your shoulders." He didn't envy Katherine and the tough decisions she was going to have to make. Sadie and Ida were both set in their ways and weren't about to

Silver in the Moonlight

let someone else tell them how to run their lives. "I'll be here if you need help in any way, or someone to just listen to you."

"Why are you being so nice? Free shoulders to lean on, expert medical treatment, and free coffee. What gives?"

"Just part of that famous Southern hospitality." He shrugged when he noticed the skeptical gleam in her eyes. "Okay, so I happen to care what happens to Sadie and Ida, is that so terrible?" He didn't like spelling out his every emotion. He had been raised by very proper and reserved parents, a string of cold nannies, and a rigid prep school. Emotions were something you felt in private.

"No, Dean, that isn't terrible." Katherine gave him a funny little smile that did incredible things to his stomach. "Actually I think it's quite sweet of you."

The last thing he wanted was for her to think he was sweet. Little girls were sweet. Ice cream was sweet. Sadie and Ida were sweet. He would prefer Katherine to think he was strong, or intelligent, or wonderful, or even sensitive. But not sweet. "Bankers are never *sweet*, Katherine. It would ruin our reputation."

She placed her empty cup in the sink. "What reputation would that be, Dean? The one regarding foreclosing on widows and orphans?"

He didn't like that mischievous look that once again gleamed in her eyes. He'd wager everything in his wallet that Katherine Silver had given her parents more than a few rough lessons in child rearing. His cup joined hers. "I've never once foreclosed on a widow or an orphan."

"Like I said, you're sweet." She glanced at the kitchen clock and the teasing glint in her eyes faded. "You're going to be late for work."

He looked at the clock with a sense of surprise. Katherine was right. He was going to be late for work, and for once in his life he really didn't care. Shelia Parker, his secretary, had a key to the bank, and she knew the combination to the safe. Shelia was trained to fill in for him, even though the opportunities were few and far between. It would do her good to be thrown off balance by his lateness. Besides, he would much rather share a cup of coffee and a morning conversation with Katherine than face the pile of paperwork on his desk. "What good is it to be the boss if you can't be late once in a while?"

"Well, I guess being the boss has some advantages, but I still don't want you getting into trouble on my behalf." She headed for the back door. "Thanks for the offer of a friendly ear. I'll probably take you up on it. But definitely count on me for coffee."

"You're welcome, and please do." He crossed the room and held the screen door open for her. Her light floral scent teased his nose. "Thank Sadie and Ida for the cookies for me, will you?"

Silver in the Moonlight

"I managed to eat quite a few of them. Sorry about that."

"No problem. It saves me from tacking on more mileage."

"That's great for you, but what am I supposed to do?"

"You can always go jogging with me in the morning. I could use the company." It wasn't exactly how he wanted to see Katherine, pounding the pavement with him and all out of breath, but he'd take her company any way he could get it.

"No offense, Dean, but I'd rather have all my fingernails yanked out than go jogging." She passed through the door and out onto the veranda. "You'd better hightail it to work before someone fires you."

He watched her head back over to her aunts' house. This time she walked around the fence to the front of the house instead of squeezing through the thorn-guarded opening. He wasn't worried about being fired, or even reprimanded. He owned the damn bank. What did worry him was that he hadn't cared that he was going to be late.

He should have been tripping over his feet and rushing for the door, hustling her out ahead of him. He should be rushing right now instead of just standing there watching the graceful sway of Katherine's hips and admiring the way her navy-blue shorts clung to her bottom.

So why wasn't he?

With a rueful shake of his head he stepped back into the kitchen and finished getting ready for work. No one was there to see him swipe the last two cookies from the plate as he headed out the door.

THREE

"Isn't this just lovely!" Sadie exclaimed as she spread the plaid blanket beneath a massive oak tree. "We haven't been here in years, Kitty. This was a wonderful idea."

Katherine smiled as she lowered the loaded picnic basket to the ground. The thing weighed a ton. Sadie had to have packed enough food for a weekend retreat instead of a simple picnic lunch. "I thought you two would appreciate a change of scenery."

"It's so peaceful and beautiful out here," Ida said.

She had to agree with her aunts. Molly's Park gave a spectacular view of the Combahee River to the east. The idea of getting her aunts away from the house had come to her about two hours after leaving Dean's that morning. She had tried to talk to them at home, but both had been distracted by things that needed to be done, a pie that had to be baked, or a weed that had to be pulled. Getting them away from the house for a quiet afternoon might be the key to communicating with them.

She helped Ida and Sadie sit down on the blanket in the shade. "Now you two get a chance to relax for a while."

"We relax all the time, Kitty," Sadie said.

"Well, you could have fooled me. I haven't seen you sit down for more than five minutes since I arrived. Even last night at dinner, you both kept popping up to get something else." She smiled at her aunts to soften her words. "I think you two need to slow down a little."

Sadie gave an indignant huff and looked away. Ida frowned. "You sound just like Dean."

Katherine reached for one of Ida's and one of Sadie's hands, holding them gently. She loved her aunts dearly and wouldn't hurt them for anything in the world, but this was important. "Maybe Dean's right. Did you two ever think of that?"

"And maybe he's wrong," Sadie muttered, still not looking at her.

"We like Dean very much," Ida said. "He's a good boy and a fine neighbor." She pulled her hand out of Katherine's grasp and plucked at a tall stem of grass next to the blanket. "It's not so much Dean that upsets us."

"It's not? What's upsetting you, then?"

"They want to put us in a home and take our

house away from us." Ida's thin fingers ripped the grass out by its roots.

"That house was our father's, and his father's before him, and his father's before him." Sadie appeared to be on the verge of tears. "Hamilton said the house was ours for as long as we wanted it."

Katherine felt as if someone had just kicked her in the stomach. She hadn't realized Sadie and Ida knew about Dean's ridiculous notion of putting them in River View Rest Home. Then again, Ida had said "*they* want to put us in a home," not "*he* wants to put us in a home." "Who wants to put you in a home?"

"Everyone, Katherine." Ida yanked out another tuft of grass.

"Who's everyone? I want names." This was worse than she had thought. She was going to murder someone. She wasn't sure who until she had some names. Lots of names.

Sadie finally met her gaze. "You won't let them take our home, will you, Kitty?" Behind her glasses, tears filled her faded blue eyes, and suddenly Sadie looked every one of her seventy-four years. "It's going to be your home one day. Little Edward wants nothing to do with it, so we decided to leave it to you when our time comes."

Katherine could feel tears burning in the back of her own eyes. "Don't talk like that, Sadie. You two are going to be around for a long, long time." She gave Sadie's ample body a hug, then pulled Ida into her arms. She could feel the slight trembling of her aunt's lean body. "No one is going to take your home." She kissed Ida's cheek. "I promise."

She couldn't believe this! Dean had been so sweet and caring toward her aunts. If he had anything to do with this she'd make him wish he'd never laid eyes on Ida or Sadie Silver. She'd start with dumping his delicious caffeine-loaded coffee over his head and then she'd get nasty. Real nasty.

Sadie and Ida were both looking at her as if she was suddenly wearing tights, a red cape, and a big letter *S* on her chest. She wasn't hero material, but she'd be damned before she'd allow anyone to run her aunts out of their house and into a rest home. "Now tell me who threatened to take your house and put you in nursing home?"

Sadie glanced at Ida. "They didn't really threaten us, Kitty. They suggested we might be more comfortable in a, let's see . . . what did they call it, Ida?"

"An assisted-living community." Ida's voice broke with each word.

"Who are 'they'?" Katherine prayed Dean's name wouldn't pass their lips. She liked Dean, and not just because he was gorgeous and made delicious coffee. He had honestly seemed concerned for Sadie and Ida's welfare. She could overlook his fetish with medical supplies and

Silver in the Moonlight

scratches if she just considered it further proof of his caring nature.

"Mostly it's the Revitalization of Jasper Committee," Sadie answered.

"Who and what is the Revitalization of Jasper Committee?" It sounded like a group of retired butlers trying to get back into the workforce.

"Jasper has been doing a lot of renovations to bring in tourists." Ida gave her a funny look. "Didn't you notice all the fancy new shops on Main Street?"

"To tell you the truth, no." Katherine tried to appear apologetic. "Once I hit Jasper I just zipped on down Main until I reached Jackson Avenue."

"Oh my." Sadie sighed. "They won't like that."

"Who are *they*?" Sadie made it sound as if the entire town of Jasper was being controlled by aliens.

"The committee," Sadie said.

Katherine refused to groan or show any other sign of being disturbed at her aunts' lack of understanding. She wanted names. She needed names. "Who's on this noble committee to bring tourists to Jasper?"

She knew about tourism. She had worked as a travel agent for the past five years. She had booked dozens of trips to Charleston for her clients and even a handful to Beaufort. But never once had anyone requested a vacation to Jasper.

As far as she knew, the travel industry had never heard of Jasper, South Carolina. Whoever was on this committee was not only bullying her aunts—they were doing a lousy job of promoting tourism.

"I think our minister is on the committee," Ida said. "He mentioned something to me at our covered-dish dinner the other week about keeping the people in Jasper working, and bringing in new families. He said tourism is not only good for our economy, but for our congregation." Ida looked at Sadie. "Remember Mabel's three-bean casserole she brought to the dinner?"

"Of course I remember. How could I forget it? It was the best thing she ever made." Sadie looked thoughtful. "For the life of me, I can't figure out what she used to give it such an interesting flavor. I asked her twice, but she wouldn't tell me." Sadie hmmphed and started unloading the picnic basket. "And to think I even gave her my Kris Kringle cookie recipe last Christmas."

"Violet told me an interesting story about Mabel's three-bean casserole."

"What?"

"Turns out she didn't make it after all. Her granddaughter and family were visiting, and before she left, the granddaughter whipped up the casserole for our church dinner."

"I knew it! I knew Mabel couldn't have made something that delicious!"

Sadie and Ida continued to discuss the apparently unskilled-in-the-kitchen Mabel and another half-dozen questionable dishes that had graced their church's dinner. Katherine allowed their voices to drone on. Even if she had gotten only one name, she knew what her first order of business was. Find this revitalization committee and have a few very direct words with its chairman.

Katherine couldn't believe it. She had been asked to leave the kitchen, politely, yet firmly. Sadie and Ida had their routine down pat and her presence was disturbing them, they said. Great, she thought. She'd been relegated to wandering through the house for the next hour while her two elderly aunts prepared her dinner. There was definitely something wrong with this picture, but for the life of her she couldn't figure out how to change it. Both Sadie and Ida refused to listen to her. She had given up the argument when Sadie got all misty-eyed and said the day she couldn't prepare dinner for three people was the day she'd hang up her apron and check herself into a rest home. How could Katherine have argued against that statement?

She left the kitchen after informing her aunts she was taking them out for dinner the following night and there would be no arguing about it.

Meanwhile she had some time to kill. It was a perfect opportunity to do some snooping. She looked around the front hall and did a double take when she noticed the back wall. A large gold-framed mirror hung above a table draped with lace, upon which sat a huge vase of flowers. It was a beautiful arrangement, but it caught her eye because it wasn't centered properly. Table and mirror both were a good foot too far to the right.

She remembered Dean's warning that Sadie and Ida had a tendency to hide needed repairs. She walked over to the mirror and peeked behind it. An ugly brown water stain ran from ceiling to floor. It was a good twelve inches wide and a hideous shade of brown against the creamy yellow wall. The roof leaked, or had leaked in the past. Either way, Sadie and Ida hadn't bothered to repair the wall and repaint. She had to wonder if they had bothered to repair the roof. The sagging roof.

She walked around the front parlor looking for more signs of neglect, and finding them. Two of the windows had cracked panes and one wouldn't open. Pictures and furniture were strategically placed to cover cracked plaster. Even the couch and chairs were in need of reupholstering, at the least. The wood tables and the secretary tucked neatly into the corner shone with a recent polishing. Two vases held eye-catching arrangements of brilliantly colored flowers. Still, the room held a certain sadness.

Her aunts' old and quaint house wasn't so quaint after all. Doilies hid worn patches on the

Silver in the Moonlight

chairs and couch. Drapes were pulled back, not to let more light into the room, but because one of the window frames was rotting and leaking. The back room, which Sadie and Ida referred to as the sitting room, was in the same dismal shape.

The formal dining room had recently received a new coat of paint and a window treatment. But she knew the reason for those improvements. The missing mahogany dining table and two of its chairs were the only reminders of the New Year's Eve fire, but it was enough. She had questioned Sadie about the missing table, hoping she would come clean about the fire, but instead her aunt told her it was out being refinished. That could have been true, because she didn't know how much damage had been done to the table, so she had let the subject drop.

Sadie and Ida had done an excellent job of hiding the neglect during her other visits. She honestly hadn't seen anything wrong with the house. Now she knew what to look for and was appalled at how gullible she had been. That morning she had taken a walk around the house, telling Ida she wanted to see the gardens. In reality, she'd wanted to check the foundation.

It had been a wasted trip. She couldn't get within three feet of her goal because of the trees, shrubs, and plants. Ida had the entire house surrounded by so much dense foliage, she had begun to wonder if the trees and plants were actually holding up the house. It was going to take a lumber jack to get close enough to inspect the foundation.

The second-story porch across the back of the house looked totally unsafe and was actually tilting to the left. Three-quarters of the back veranda had been enclosed sometime in the late twenties. She'd wager the inheritance Grandfather Roland had left her that it hadn't been touched since. With a lot of money and time it could be the best room in the house. The entire back wall was made of floor-to-ceiling windows with the most incredible view of the gardens and river.

Dean was right. If Sadie and Ida didn't do something soon, the entire house just might collapse on their heads. She glanced away from the shabby room behind her and stared out the window to the river beyond. What was she going to do?

"Kitty." Sadie's voice echoed from the front hallway. "It's dinnertime."

Katherine didn't even bother to cringe at the absurd nickname as she turned from the window. She had much larger things to think about. "I'll be right there."

Hours later the clock on her bedroom bureau showed the time as just before ten o'clock. The grandfather clock in the hallway was chiming the hour of three. Katherine couldn't go to sleep yet.

Silver in the Moonlight

She hadn't even bothered to get undressed. Too many thoughts were racing around in her brain. Besides, she never went to bed before eleven. In Boston it was virtually unheard of.

Her aunts had retired nearly an hour ago. Considering their early-morning baking-and-gardening routine, she had been surprised they made it through dinner. Life in Jasper traveled at a different, slower pace. A pace her body wasn't used to. She needed to do something and rocking in the rocker in her bedroom wasn't cutting it. She needed movement. She needed space.

As quietly as she could, she crept out of the bedroom and down the stairs, avoiding the third step from the top that squeaked. In the kitchen she slipped out the back door. The moon and the river were once again calling her. Maybe the fresh air and gentle night breezes would help her think more clearly. The grass was cool under her bare feet as she made her way to the river's edge.

The moon was a huge white glowing ball in the velvety black sky, and its light shimmered across the slow-moving water. Perfect for lovers, lunatics, and werewolves. How could something be associated with both sweethearts and lunatics? she wondered. A light laugh escaped her as she thought about that. In a strange way it made sense to her. The one time in her life she had fallen in love she had turned into a raging lunatic, or so her ex-fiancé had claimed.

She had met Todd Rutledge the summer after

she graduated from college. She had honored her parents' wishes and moved back home while she looked for work and figured out the direction her life was going to take. It had been a whirlwind courtship and she was in love before she caught her breath. They were to be married in November. By the end of August the stardust hadn't just faded from her eyes, it had been ripped out. Todd didn't love her. He was marrying her to get his hands on the quarter share of the Roland Shipyard she had inherited from her maternal grandfather. She had learned that one afternoon, when she overheard him bragging to a sailing buddy how easy it was to acquire twenty-five percent of a shipyard. Todd had seen nothing wrong with the mercenary marriage, and when she confronted him he had made the error of telling her that even her parents thought it was a wonderful idea to join the Rutledge and Silver names. She had been so angry that heartbreak never entered the picture. She had asked Todd that since he was expecting to get control of her inheritance, what benefit was she to expect from this sham of a marriage. Todd had flashed his orthodontist-perfect smile and calmly, as if he were offering the Crown Jewels of England, said she would be receiving him. That was when she lost it and became a raging lunatic, as Todd so poetically put it to her parents later that night.

She glanced once again at the glowing moon and acknowledged that lunatics and lovers did

Silver in the Moonlight

have something in common. It was a real shame she couldn't remember if the moon had been full the night she told Todd what he could do with his ring, his proposal, and the rest of his life. She laughed again as she remembered the look on his face when she picked up a crystal vase filled with roses and threatened to crown him king of England.

"Did he just tell you a joke?"

Dean's voice startled her out of her memories. She turned to him, frowning in confusion. "Who?"

He glanced up at the moon. "The man in the moon." His gaze returned to her and a smile curved his mouth. "You were looking up at him and laughing."

"Oh, him." She grinned at the moon. "He told me I was a raving lunatic."

"An uncivil, grouchy, raving lunatic." He chuckled and shook his head. "They sure make women feisty up there in Boston."

"If you think I'm bad, you should see the ones that didn't go to Miss Snodgrass's School for Young Ladies."

"Miss Snodgrass's School for Young Ladies?" Dean looked like he'd just sucked on a sour pickle. "You've got to be kidding me."

"Afraid not." She loved seeing people's reaction to that name. If Dean thought it was bad, he had no idea what it had sounded like to a thirteen-year-old girl. Miss Snodgrass hadn't turned out to be that horrible, though, even if she didn't possess a sense of humor. "It ended up being one of the more interesting six weeks of my life."

"Six weeks?"

"That's how long it took before they called my father to come and get me."

"Why would they call your father to come and get you?"

"Miss Snodgrass and I didn't see eye to eye on what proper conduct was for a young lady."

"What exactly did you do?" Dean looked fascinatingly confounded by the prospect of her not being a proper young lady.

"Which time?"

"I don't know, pick one or two."

"Well, let's see. With Miss Snodgrass's School for Young Ladies I started off small and worked my way up to the grand finale. First I took bets that I could walk the three-inch ledge around the entire third floor of our dormitory." She flashed a huge grin. "Not only did I make it, but I became thirty-two dollars richer that night."

"Good Lord, you could have broken your neck!"

"Those were Miss Snodgrass's exact words. The policeman and the six firemen that responded to the emergency call said the same thing." She gave him a thoughtful look. "If I'm not mistaken, they were also my father's exact words, but it was kind of hard to understand him

Silver in the Moonlight

since he was yelling over four hundred miles of telephone line into my ear."

"I could see why he might be a bit upset, Katherine."

"He should have known I'd make it. After all, he saw me walk the peak of our house, and that was a lot higher than three stories." She frowned at the memory of the argument that escapade had launched. "That little stunt got me sent to Miss Snodgrass's. That and the stunt I pulled the week before."

"Which was?"

"That was the month I decided to join the circus. Being an enterprising kid, I found someone who was selling llamas and used every cent in my piggy bank to purchase a big-eyed beauty named Pollyanna. She was to be my act and I was going to become the world's greatest llama trainer. When she was delivered, my mother was entertaining some women's club in the back gardens, so I snuck Pollyanna into the drawing room and closed the door. It was my misfortune that fifteen minutes later my mother wanted to show off a recently purchased painting that hung over the mantel in the drawing room."

Dean chuckled. "I can almost picture that scene."

"Well, picture Pollyanna getting hungry and eating an entire vase of flowers and then being sick all over the Oriental rug that had been in my mother's family for generations."

Dean laughed a rich deep laugh that did the most peculiar thing to her stomach. She wanted to hear him laugh again. She needed to. "See, if Miss Snodgrass had your sense of humor, I would have stuck out my high-school years there and by now be the patron saint of etiquette."

"You just have to tell me what the grand finale was that got you tossed out of her school for proper ladies."

"It wasn't meant to be the grand finale. I had something bigger in mind, but it worked just as well." She chuckled at the memory. "I was just pulling a low-class stunt, you know the one, spreading glue on the teacher's chair right before she walked into the room. Anyway, Miss Snodgrass had this arrogant, nasty cat that had free rein over the entire school. Muffin was his name, and believe me, there was nothing muffin-like about this demonic feline. Everyone hated him, except Miss Snodgrass. Immediately after I spread the glue, the teacher walked in and everyone in the class was holding their breath, waiting for her to take her seat. Just at the last moment Muffin came sauntering into the room like he owned it, jumped up on the teacher's chair, and lay down. Needless to say, a vet had to be called in to tranquilize the traumatized cat while he cut him free of the chair. Muffin's right side ended up with a GI haircut and I ended up being thrown out of the school."

As she had hoped, Dean laughed again. She

Silver in the Moonlight

really loved his laughter. He laughed so hard, he had to sit down on the soft grass. She joined him. "Miss Snodgrass was still using words no 'proper' lady would dare think, let alone utter, when my father arrived that night to pick me up. Their meeting was short, but not sweet. As he ushered me out the door I was pretty sure she muttered something about Satan's spawn, but I couldn't be positive."

"How many schools were you tossed out of?" Dean wiped at the moisture in his eyes and gave her a look that held a mixture of laughter and respect.

"Four before I finally got my way."

"What was your way?"

"I wanted to stay home and go to public school." She could still remember some of the fights her parents had had over the issue. "My parents felt it was their moral and financial responsibility to send me to private school."

"Why did you want to live at home? Were you very close to your parents?"

"Not really. I was closer to my grandfather, my mother's father, who lived with us and was in poor health. He died when I was in my senior year of high school."

"You must have loved him very much."

"I did. He was the greatest. He understood me perfectly when no one else even tried." She smiled up at the sky. "He taught me how to cheat at cards, to tie a dozen different kinds of knots, and to whistle."

"He sounds like a terrific grandfather." Dean's gaze traveled the length of her bare legs. "Couldn't you sleep?"

"It's too early yet. I'm still on my Boston schedule." Heat licked at her legs where his gaze had traveled. She was wearing the same outfit she'd had on that morning when she bartered Sadie's cookies for a cup of coffee. She could still feel the slash of desire that surged up her body as he attended to the simple scratch on her thigh. Dean Katz had incredible hands. "Do you remember your grandfathers?"

"I remember one vaguely, but my other one is still alive. Grandfather Katz is eighty-seven years young and still chasing the ladies."

It was her turn to chuckle. "He sounds wonderful. Does he live nearby?"

"In Charleston, with my parents and sister, Amanda."

She detected a strained note to his voice when he mentioned his parents. Maybe she had more in common with Dean than she first thought. Her parents had tried to talk her out of breaking her engagement with Todd. They had felt he would be a good addition to the shipyard business, since she had no plans to join the family-owned company. They had been right about that, she had absolutely no desire to work at Roland Shipyard. She allowed her father to control her share and

Silver in the Moonlight

run the business as he saw fit. One thing she knew about her father, he would never harm Roland Shipyard. But even if he could control her inheritance, he could not control her life. She had moved out of her parents' home and started her own life. Her relationship with her parents was cordial at best, and often strained.

Avoiding the topic of parents, she asked, "Is your sister younger or older than you?"

"Amanda's twenty-three and works in one of my father's banks." Dean lay back and put his hands behind his head to stare up at the moon. "A brother couldn't have asked for a better kid sister. I taught her to ride her first bike, drive her first car, and how to tell the boys no."

"She sounds lucky to have you as an older brother." Leaving a good two feet between them, she lay back as well and contemplated the stars. Lord, it was quiet in Jasper. She couldn't hear anything except an occasional frog, crickets, and the cheepers farther down the bank serenading the night. It was a peaceful sound, one that soothed her soul, but not her mind. What was she going to do about her aunts, their house, and their future?

"Penny for your thoughts?" Dean's voice was warm and seductive on the night breeze.

"You can have them for free." She glanced at him. "You were right about the condition of my aunts' house. I haven't got a look at the foundation, due mostly to Ida's obsession with growing anything green, but I believe you're correct in your assumption that it's crumbling beneath their feet."

"Call an expert in, Katherine. I could recommend a few if you don't know who to call, or use the Yellow Pages. Just make sure they specialize in restoration and preservation. Sadie and Ida both love the house the way it is."

"I'll call someone tomorrow after I have another talk with them." She wondered if she should ask Dean about the Revitalization of Jasper Committee, but decided against it. She needed to do this on her own. Sadie and Ida were her problem, not Dean's.

She looked again at the man lying next to her and wondered why she felt so safe with him. He was virtually a stranger, it was the middle of the night, and basically there wasn't anyone around who would hear her if she started to scream. Sadie was hard-of-hearing, and Ida slept like the dead. Besides, she wouldn't want her aunts to come rushing to her rescue. With Dean she didn't need to be rescued. The man was a perfect gentleman. A quiet gentleman. "A penny for *your* thoughts."

Dean didn't even glance her way as he answered, "I was just lying here wondering what you would do if I kissed you."

FOUR

Dean held his breath and waited for Katherine's response. Whatever in the world had possessed him to say such a thing? Maybe it was because it was the truth. He had been thinking about kissing her since he first saw her. He had been dreaming about doing a lot more than kissing her. Lord, no woman had ever affected him this way before. He broke out in a cold sweat just thinking about her. And now he had gone and blown it by saying something stupid.

He couldn't bear to face her, so he continued to stare up at the stars, but he wasn't really seeing them. He was picturing Katherine as she had been when he first noticed her by the river. She had looked so lonely and sad standing in the moonlight that he had immediately started toward her. Before he made it to her side, her light laugh had reached his ears and captured his heart.

He not only found Katherine attractive, but intriguing as well. It had been a long time since he'd felt desire for a woman. Maybe that was why the need to kiss her seemed so intense, so vital. For the first time in his adult life he was unsure of himself with a woman. He couldn't read Katherine's mind and had absolutely no idea how she was going to respond to his admission that he wanted to kiss her. For a while that morning, in his kitchen, he had been positive she felt the same wild attraction he was feeling. As quickly as the heat of passion had blazed in her eyes, though, it had disappeared and she had asked for a cup of coffee.

She was quiet for so long, he began to think she must have fallen asleep. Wasn't that a wonderful boost for his ego?

"I think I would like that very much." Her answer, when it finally came, was a soft whisper in the night.

He felt every muscle in his body tighten with need as he released the breath he hadn't known he was holding. He felt like an inexperienced sixteen-year-old kid, not a thirty-four-year-old man who had kissed his fair share of women. So why was his heart pounding so wildly, it seemed to want to break out of his chest?

He rolled onto his side, toward Katherine, and supported himself on his elbow. The clear

Silver in the Moonlight

skies and full moon gave him enough light to see the desire gleaming in her eyes and the seductive temptation of her waiting mouth. Lord, she was gorgeous.

With one hand he brushed away from her cheek a blonde curl being tossed by the light breeze. "I've never kissed an uncivilized grouch before."

A smile played at the corner of her mouth. "I've never kissed a banker before."

He chuckled as his finger traced the delicate curve of her jaw. "I guess that makes us even." Her skin felt like silk, warm silk. She looked so inviting, lying on the grass gazing up at him, waiting for his kiss. Waiting for him. He felt his finger tremble as he traced her moist full lower lip. "I've been waiting a long time to kiss you, Katherine."

Lord, the woman had a mouth molded for sin and all he had to do was lower his head to taste her sweetness. His gut clenched against the onslaught of desire ripping through his body. He wanted to go slow and easy with her, but he was afraid that once he tasted Katherine, a kiss wouldn't be enough.

She smiled bewitchingly. "I only got here yesterday."

He lost the battle before it had even begun. "What in the hell took you so long?" he muttered, before lowering his head and claiming her mouth.

Katherine felt herself stretch up to meet Dean's mouth. The man certainly took a long time to kiss a woman. She had been waiting for his kiss since that morning in his kitchen. Heat slammed into her body as his mouth slanted across hers with the expertise of a certified rogue. She closed her eyes and fell into the kiss.

Desire kindled, blazed, and raged from where her lips meshed with his to the tips of her Raspberry Delight–painted toenails. Dean's tongue swept across her lips in an appeal for entrance. She complied and wrapped her arms around his neck to pull him closer.

The weight and warmth of Dean's upper body blocked the pleasantly cool evening air as if he were an inferno. An inferno she willingly joined as the kiss deepened. Their tongues danced and volleyed in a rhythm as old as time. Heat built and all the reasons she had told herself why she shouldn't be attracted to her aunts' next-door neighbor were incinerated by the blaze.

She wanted Dean with an intensity that should have surprised her, but somehow didn't. Casual sex wasn't her style, but there was nothing casual about the way Dean was kissing her. With every thrust of his tongue he sent her deeper into the heat. Her heart was pounding furiously against her ribs, her bones seemed to be melting, and her breasts felt swollen, the nipples sensitive to the lace they were pushing against. She wanted Dean's touch.

Silver in the Moonlight

He released her mouth and pressed a string of moist kisses over her jaw and down her throat. His words were muffled as he spoke against the sensitive area where her neck curved into a shoulder. "Sweet Katherine, I do want you."

She felt his hand slip under the hem of her shirt. Sparks flared where his fingers stroked. She couldn't prevent the low moan that escaped her throat as his hand slid higher until he cupped her breast. He captured the tail end of her moan with his hungry mouth. Her fingers wove through his hair and tugged him closer. She wanted him closer. Close enough for her to crawl right into him and keep this spectacular feeling forever.

It took Dean two tries before he released the front clasp of her bra. His sigh of pleasure as her soft breast overflowed his palm mingled with hers. Katherine tasted like sin. She tasted better than Sadie's chocolate-chip cookies straight from the oven. He was in trouble.

Deep trouble.

But he already knew that. He'd known that morning as they'd stood in his kitchen playfully bantering over a plate of cookies. He'd known the night before as they'd walked through Ida's gardens, surrounded by moonlight. Hell, he'd known he was in trouble yesterday afternoon when she whizzed up Sadie and Ida's driveway like a race-car driver trying to qualify for the Indianapolis 500.

Katherine Silver was a five-foot-seven-inch

package of trouble. Tempting, delicious, sexy trouble. He'd sooner stop breathing than give up on such a seductive package of trouble.

He brushed his thumb over the stiff peak of her breast and groaned with pleasure as she nipped his lower lip. Arching her back, she thrust herself more fully into his palm. His arousal behind the zipper of his jeans grew more painful with her every whimper, her every movement. He nearly stopped breathing altogether when her bare thigh pressed against the front of his pants.

His control was slipping faster than every one of his good intentions. He had to taste her, just this once. He had to know if his dreams from the previous night were anywhere close to reality. He pulled her shirt up and broke the kiss. His gaze caressed her full pale breasts topped with dusky circles and taut nipples.

Slowly, so slowly that he could almost hear Katherine's frustration mount, he lowered his mouth and circled one nipple with his tongue. Katherine's fingers weren't gentle as she tugged his head closer and pressed herself deeper into his mouth.

The best wines, the choicest cuts of meat, or the sweetest chocolates couldn't have tasted finer. Her nipple grew harder as he pulled it deep within his mouth and laved it with his tongue. His arousal pushed against her thigh as he released the one breast and captured its twin. Her hips pressed into his in a tantalizing rhythm, and

Silver in the Moonlight

he willed himself to regain control of the situation.

All he had wanted was to compare the taste of her breasts with his dreams. He had done that. He now knew his dreams hadn't even come close to the real thing. Katherine was far more dangerous than he had thought. Katherine tasted like forever.

He slowly released the quivering nipple and regretfully refastened her bra. It took him four tries before the simple plastic clasp caught and held. U-shaped wire and white lace lifted, molded, and compressed the pale mounds into an eye-popping shape that overflowed the scalloped edges of lace.

"Dean?"

The trembling in Katherine's husky voice tore at his heart. She sounded as confused and bewildered as he felt. He lowered her shirt and brushed her hair away from her flushed face. "I had to stop, Katherine."

Looking over his shoulder, she pushed herself away from him and sat up. She smoothed her hair with shaking fingers as she stared at the river. "I understand, Dean. Thank you."

"Don't thank me and please don't say you understand when I don't."

She shot him a look from the corner of her eye. "What don't you understand?"

"Why I know it's so damned right to stop

before we go any further when I ache for you clear to my back teeth."

Katherine's "Ohhh . . ." faded into the night. She tugged her shirt down farther as he sat up next to her. "You were right, Dean. We needed to stop."

"What we needed was a more private place, a box of condoms, and a big feather bed." He caressed her cheek. "We also needed time, Katherine. Once I get you into my bed, I'm not letting you out for at least a week, possibly two."

"Oh, my!"

The expression on her face was priceless. She looked appalled, embarrassed, and excited by his declaration.

He laughed. "You can say that again."

She playfully fanned herself with her hand, and using a Southern accent that dripped with honey, she murmured, "Oh, my sweet Lord . . ."

He stood up, reached for her hand, and helped her to her feet. "Come on, trouble. It's way past your bedtime." He started walking toward her aunts' house. The faster he got her inside the house, the sooner he would be able to breathe easier. Desire was still pumping through his veins, but at least his head was clearing.

He slowed his stride when he noticed that Katherine had to take two steps for every one of his. Ida's garden was so wild that for part of the way Katherine had to walk behind him instead of alongside of him. Usually the thick fragrance of the flowers was enough to gag him, but that night all he could smell was the light vanilla scent of Katherine's perfume. Even her hair smelled of vanilla. It was a cruel fragrance to wear around a man who was constantly hungry, and not just for food.

He stopped at the foot of the stairs leading to the small back porch. The stairs were only three feet wide, but Ida had placed a huge clay pot on one end of every step. Petunias in a rainbow of colors flowed from one pot to the next like a floral waterfall. He brushed a kiss across Katherine's forehead and gently pushed her toward the stairs. "You'd better go in before I change my mind."

She gave him a look he couldn't interpret. "Could I make you change your mind?"

"Without even trying, Kate." He prodded her once again toward the steps and was relieved when she stepped up onto the first one. "I'll put on the coffee before my run tomorrow, so if you want a cup just make yourself at home. I'll leave the kitchen door open for you." He wanted to make sure she wasn't going to go into hiding come daybreak. He knew her weakness for coffee and wasn't afraid to use it.

She walked up onto the porch, then looked at him and asked, "Do you own a feather bed?"

He suppressed a groan as a heated ball of desire slammed into his gut. "No, but I'll have one delivered by tomorrow afternoon." Seeing Kate snuggled in the middle of a big old-fashioned feather bed with an expression of total satisfaction on her face would be well worth the cost. And since when had he started seeing her as a "Kate" instead of the more demure Katherine?

She stepped farther into the darkness of the porch. "Suit yourself, Dean, but there is one thing you should know about me."

He heard more than saw the screen door open. "What's that?" There were a lot of things he wanted to know about Kate. The first being, would she make that little moaning sound, like she had when he tugged on her nipples, when he was deep inside her? That question alone was going to cost him an entire night's sleep.

Her whisper traveled on the night breeze as she opened the door and stepped inside. "I'm allergic to down."

Dean chuckled as the door closed softly behind her. She was allergic to feathers. Well, hell, there went his fantasy about her wearing nothing but a black boa and a killer smile.

Katherine sat at Dean's kitchen table and savored her first sip of coffee of the day. Dean made one mean cup of coffee. She had once again been summoned to deliver the baked goods of the day to him. This morning Sadie was producing bread, cinnamon raisin bread. Dean's loaf was sitting on a plate on the table, covered by a linen napkin. She had knocked on his kitchen door but hadn't received an answer. She had been about to head back to her aunts, but the aroma of freshly brewed coffee and his invitation from the night before were too tempting. When she stepped into the kitchen she heard water running somewhere on the second floor. Dean was taking a shower. The man was entirely too trusting. Whoever heard of leaving your door unlocked while you took a shower? Hadn't the man ever seen *Psycho*?

She stared into the dark coffee in her cup and thought about Dean's powerful, lean body being pounded by the spray of the shower. Last night she had lain in bed for a long time staring at the ceiling and going over every word, every move, and every kiss they had shared. She had also spent an abundance of time thinking about his body.

One question had kept repeating itself far into the night. Why had he stopped? She remembered his words. He'd said he had to stop. But why? She had been so caught up in the moment, she hadn't even thought about stopping. Heck, she hadn't been thinking at all, she had been feeling.

Lord, where had all that heat come from? One minute she had been contemplating what it would feel like to share a kiss with her aunts' gorgeous next-door neighbor and the next minute she had been engulfed in a torrent of heat so powerful, it would have fried her socks if she had been wearing any. No man had ever kissed her like that. She hadn't known it was possible.

The other question that had haunted her all night long was what was she going to do about Dean, and this obviously mutual attraction. She gave a rueful chuckle as she glanced around his kitchen. Sadie, once again, hadn't given her a whole lot of options that morning. It was either deliver his bread or hurt the feelings of her seventy-four-year-old aunt. She wouldn't hurt Sadie's feelings for all the cinnamon bread in the world. So there she sat drinking Dean's coffee and wondering what he looked like naked. Life, sometimes, just wasn't fair.

"Ah . . . I see you found the coffee." Dean stepped into the kitchen carrying his suit jacket, tie, and a pair of black shoes so shiny, she could see the reflection of his hand in them.

She lifted her cup in a mock salute and couldn't help smiling. Lord, he was sexy with his hair all damp from the shower and his face freshly shaven. "I followed my nose."

He draped his jacket and tie on the back of one of the kitchen chairs, dropped his shoes to the floor, and headed for the coffeepot. "Let me guess." He nodded toward the linen-covered plate sitting in the middle of his table. "Bread?"

"That was too easy. The shape gave it away." She finished her coffee and set the empty cup in front of her. "What kind of bread?"

Dean leaned over her shoulder and sniffed the air. "Cinnamon."

Silver in the Moonlight

"Cinnamon what?" She was amazed at herself for playing this silly guessing game with him. She should be totally embarrassed, or at least uneasy with Dean. So why wasn't she? It felt perfectly normal to be sitting in his kitchen drinking his coffee. In fact, she was beginning to wonder how his morning kisses would compare with his night kisses.

"Cinnamon nut?"

"Nope."

"Cinnamon apple?"

"If your next guess is wrong I get to take it back to Sadie." Heaven only knew what her aunt would do with another loaf of bread. Sadie already had a half dozen cooling in her own kitchen.

"Cinnamon raisin!"

Dean looked so proud of himself when she nodded that she couldn't resist returning his smile. He must have had his poor mother wrapped around his finger when he was a little boy. "You better hurry up and get some breakfast. I wouldn't want to make you late for a second day in a row."

Dean grabbed a bowl and box of cereal that promised to give you one hundred percent of your daily allowance of every vitamin and mineral known to mankind. "Want some?"

She shuddered. Seven-day-old hamster food held more appeal to her. "No, thanks. I've been sitting here smelling your CARE package and drooling."

Dean chuckled and handed her a plate, knife, and a tub of margarine that had no fat, no cholesterol, and basically no taste. The only nice thing she could say about it was that it was the color of real butter. "Help yourself."

She sliced into the bread and figured any unhealthy food Dean ate came from next door. Sadie and Ida always had honest-to-goodness real butter in their refrigerator. Sweet, creamy, artery-clogging butter. She wasn't much better when it came to her diet. She still preferred presweetened kid's cereal to anything that looked even remotely "good for you," and considered herself blessed if the box came with marshmallows and a free toy.

She spread the margarine on thick and watched as it melted into the warm bread. "So how's the banking business? Did you foreclose on any orphans or widows yesterday?"

"Not yesterday, but with any luck something will turn up today." Dean poured skim milk over his cereal and started to eat.

Well, at least the man had a sense of humor. Obviously his sense of taste was all screwed up. Who could eat those tiny balls of cardboard floating in his bowl and not choke? "I took Sadie and Ida on a picnic yesterday afternoon to Molly's Park."

"Did you see the ghost?"

Silver in the Moonlight

"No. Sadie told me you can only see Molly's ghost on rainy nights." She had been fascinated, and saddened, by the legend of poor Molly. Molly Lemont had been the daughter of the wealthiest businessman in town. When she was sixteen she had fallen in love with a local boy. They would meet secretly in the park because her father didn't approve of the boy. Then the Civil War had broken out and the boy, like all the other boys, joined the Confederate army. The day he was leaving to join his unit they agreed to meet one last time.

Their parting was tearful. The boy promised to return and make her his wife. Molly promised to wait for him. She never made it more than two hundred feet from their rendezvous spot. It had been a rainy afternoon. Her horse lost his footing and she tumbled from the saddle, breaking her neck and dying instantly. Rumor had it the young soldier died at Gettysburg. Molly's ghost was supposedly haunting the park, waiting for his return.

She wondered if Dean had ever seen Molly's ghost. "Do you think Molly's still waiting for her beau?" It was a romantic, tragic legend. One thing she was learning about the South was that every place had a story behind it or a legend connected to it.

"I think Molly's dead."

So much for him having a romantic soul. "What about all the people who have seen her?"

"The only ones who go out to Molly's Park at night are teenagers, and they go there to make out or party. I'm not sure how reliable their word is." Dean finished his cereal and reached for a piece of bread.

"Ida said she saw something that looked like it might have been Molly's ghost back in the early thirties."

Dean raised an eyebrow and grinned. "I always knew Ida was a party animal."

"Dean, you're talking about my dear sweet aunt, whom I love very much."

"I'm talking about Ida Silver, the same sweet woman who told Jesse Hopkins last week that Confederate soldiers were sneaking into her garden at night and stealing flowers."

Katherine instantly defended her aunt. "Maybe someone *is* cutting her flowers." She had no idea how Ida could possibly keep track of all the flowers blooming in the yard. There had to be over a hundred different varieties, and thousands blooming at the same time. The climbing jasmine and weeping wisteria alone were enough to keep Martha Stewart busy for a year.

"Who would be stealing Ida's flowers? She gives them away by the vaseful." Dean refilled both their cups with the remaining coffee and started to put his shoes on. "And how do you explain the Confederate soldiers?"

She drank the coffee he'd just poured only

because it was so dang good. Dean obviously still thought Ida was one short step away from River View Rest Home. He thought wrong. "Just because Ida gets confused sometimes doesn't mean she's senile."

"I didn't say she was senile, Kate. I like Ida very much. I just don't believe she, or anyone else for that matter, saw the ghost of Molly Lemont."

"Fine, there are no such things as ghosts." She polished off her coffee and stood. She really didn't want to discuss poor Molly, or any other ghost. "Who's on the Revitalization of Jasper Committee?"

Dean's head seemed to snap up. "You mean now?"

"Yes, now." Why did he have that peculiar look on his face?

"Why do you want to know?" He bent down and finished tying his shoe, then stood and slipped the tie underneath the collar of his white shirt.

"Because they are trying to toss my aunts out of their house." She watched Dean closely as he knotted the tie without the aid of a mirror. Did he seem a little edgy, or was it her imagination?

"They aren't trying to kick your aunts out of their own house, Kate."

She usually didn't like her name being shortened to any of its various nicknames, but for some reason, when Dean called her Kate it sounded intimate. Last night he had called her Kate. "Sadie and Ida say they are."

"I say they aren't. The committee doesn't have the power to make people leave their homes. Nor do they want to." Dean walked out of the kitchen and into the front hall to straighten his tie in front of a mirror. "Their only job is to make Jasper more attractive and convenient for tourists."

She followed him into the hall. "Well, they're doing a lousy job at it." Why was he sticking up for the committee and naturally assuming that Sadie and Ida were misreading the situation?

Dean's fingers froze in the middle of straightening his tie. "What do you mean?"

"They might have prettied up the town and made it more convenient for tourists, but the tourists won't come."

"Why not?"

"Because the tourist industry has never heard of Jasper, South Carolina." It made such perfect sense to her, she couldn't imagine why no one else had figured it out. "If the travel agents don't know about Jasper, how do you expect them to 'sell' the town to clients?"

Dean looked pensive. "How do you know travel agents don't know about Jasper?"

"Because I happen to be one."

"You're a travel agent?"

She shrugged. He didn't have to sound so dis-

Silver in the Moonlight

believing. "I've got to eat." That wasn't necessarily true. Grandfather Roland had left her enough to live comfortably for the rest of her life, but she knew she'd be crazy within six months if all she did all day and night was flit around Boston like some social butterfly. Being a travel agent suited her. She liked the profession, although lately she had been getting tired of seeing to everyone else's dreams when her own were still unfulfilled.

He smiled. "So you really are a travel agent."

"I could probably quote you prices on airfare and hotel accommodations for any major city. I can make travel arrangements for your pet and I can even find you a certain-colored suite at a hotel."

"A certain-colored suite?"

"I have a wealthy client who insists she can't sleep unless the color scheme in her bedroom is yellow. So far I've managed to book all her vacations in exactly the city she requested."

"Sounds complicated."

Katherine rolled her eyes. "You have no idea." She went back into the kitchen and loaded the dishes in the dishwasher as Dean put everything else away. He was going to be late again if he didn't hurry. "Since this committee has been seeking to attract tourists, I would imagine there's a pretty good restaurant in town."

"There are a couple of good restaurants in the

area. What are you looking for? Good simple food, elegant, romantic?" He slipped on his jacket.

"Elegant, I guess. I'm taking Sadie and Ida out tonight. They refuse to allow me into the kitchen except to eat. I figure I'll give them the night off."

"Try Lucinda's. Sadie and Ida would like it there. The food is excellent and the atmosphere is pure Southern charm."

Her aunts liked and respected Dean. Maybe if he reassured them that this famed committee wasn't trying to take their home away, they would believe him. On impulse, she asked, "Would you like to come along?" Dean also could lend her some support when she mentioned calling in a contractor to inspect the foundation of the house and to see what else needed to be done to make the place safer and comfortable. Installing central air and seeing to the leaking roof were top priorities.

Dean smiled. "I thought you would never ask."

She opened the screen door and stepped out onto the porch. "Seven okay?"

"Seven's fine." He closed the door behind them and locked it.

"Plan to be used." She didn't want Dean to think there were any romantic intentions in the invitation. She also wanted him to know what he might be walking into.

Silver in the Moonlight

"Used by three lovely women? Jasper would be scandalized."

"I'm going to use you to convince my aunts to let me call in a contractor to inspect their house."

They walked to the end of his drive, where he would turn left to walk to the bank and she would turn right, toward her aunts' yard. Dean leaned forward and pressed a fleeting kiss to her forehead. "I'll help with your aunts any way that I can, Kate. But I think they will listen to you before anyone else. I tried to approach that subject once before and was politely, and with a great deal of charm, told to mind my own business."

"Could I keep you as a kind of backup for my arguments?" She noticed Dean had stared at her mouth for an awfully long time before pressing that brotherly kiss onto her forehead. What had happened to the heat from last night? Was he regretting straying over the line of their budding friendship? It was difficult to tell. This morning he was a friend and nothing more. She wasn't sure if she liked this Ping-Ponging back and forth. In fact, she knew she didn't like it.

"You can use me for a backup anytime you wish, Kate."

She stretched up on her toes, cupped his face in both hands, and planted a kiss on his mouth that was guaranteed to scorch his fancy banker's shorts. She kissed him long enough to feel the beginning of his response before breaking off and stepping back. His eyes were glazed and his breathing was rapid. Good, she thought. Now he was in the same condition she was: frustrated.

She had to clear her throat twice before speaking. "I'll see you tonight at seven." Without waiting for an answer, she turned and walked up the shell driveway of her aunts' house. That, she thought with satisfaction, should put an end to any ideas of friendship he might be harboring.

FIVE

Katherine stood in front of the cheval glass, putting on her pearl earrings and stepping into her shoes. When she had packed for this trip to Jasper, she had brought mostly casual summer clothes, and only a couple dressy outfits. The yellow dress she was now wearing was one of her favorites. It wasn't warm enough up in Boston to wear it yet, but May in South Carolina was the perfect temperature.

With its short sleeves and scoop neckline, the attractive dress made her feel and look feminine, a fact she wanted to bring to Dean's attention. Since she was being honest with herself, she knew the dress looked to be tailor-made for her. When she was little her mother had refused to dress her in yellow because of her light blonde hair. Now that she bought her own clothes, she managed to have more than her fair share of yellow in her closet.

She turned in front of the mirror, critically studying her reflection. She looked good. But was it good enough for Dean to think twice before placing another brotherly kiss on her brow? His parting kiss from that morning had irked her all day long. Fortunately, more than a few household chores had needed her attention.

All afternoon she had helped Ida thin out the jasmine overtaking the exterior walls of the house. She also had been subtly pumping her aunt for information. She had done the same that morning when she helped Sadie put up twenty-four pints of strawberry jam. Ida didn't like the gardens nearly wild, but she was getting up there in age and didn't know how to ask for help. Sadie loved baking and cooking, though she knew she didn't need to go to such extremes. She was afraid of having nothing to do all day, however, so she kept the neighbors in baked goods. It was her way of feeling needed.

By four o'clock Ida and Katherine had stopped for the day and met Sadie under the towering oak deep in the backyard, close to the river. Sadie had prepared freshly squeezed lemonade and cookies to nibble on. The river provided the view and a cool breeze. Both of her aunts were looking forward to dinner at Lucinda's and were as giddy as a pair of schoolgirls. With their spirits high and their daily work behind them, she

Silver in the Moonlight

brought up the subject of having the house inspected. She had been expecting an argument. Instead she got silence and then a muttered, "We'll think about it." She considered it a good sign. She hoped that with Dean's help, that night, she could get them to agree.

Dean's help. She liked the sound of that. It was comforting to know she had someone who was willing to help her with her aunts. Their own nephew, her father, wouldn't so much as call them once a year and wish them a merry Christmas. Dean had given her one of his broad shoulders to lean on. It was a reassuring thought.

Thinking of Dean made her hurry through the rest of her preparations. She fastened on the gold watch her parents had given her for her last birthday, sprayed on some perfume, picked up her purse, and headed for the bedroom door.

Sadie and Ida were both still in their bedrooms getting ready. She knocked first on Sadie's door and then on Ida's, giving them the same message. "I'm going over to get Dean. We'll be back in a few minutes."

She hurried down the stairs and out the front door. As she crossed the drive she glanced at the garage that housed her aunts' automobile. She really didn't feel like driving the '56 Buick to Lucinda's, but she didn't have a choice. Her little MG was a two-seater. The Buick was a boat, complete with fins and a steering wheel that could pilot the *Queen Mary*. It had made it to

Molly's Park with barely a backfire. Of course it had taken two hands and all of her strength to turn the thing, as well as both feet on the brake to make it stop. She couldn't figure out how Sadie managed to drive the thing to church every Sunday and to the grocery store once a week.

She hadn't made it halfway down the drive when Dean stepped around the end of the rose-covered fence and into the yard. He was wearing a different suit than the one he'd had on that morning. This one was gray and he looked incredibly sexy in it. Of course, he had looked sexy that morning too. If she had known bankers were such great kissers, she would have paid more attention to them in Boston when her parents kept, not so subtly, introducing her to them. She always had the impression that bankers were nerdy, pompous individuals who never smiled and counted stacks of money all day. Dean could break every one of those misconceptions with just his smile.

"My, don't you look spiffy." She waited for him to join her by the rose barrier separating her aunts' property from his. The fragrant pink blooms were bigger than her fist and so plentiful, the entire fence appeared pink. She hadn't retaliated against the thorny barrier yet, but it was on her list. Ida would have a heart attack if she suggested giving the rosebushes a crew cut in the middle of their blooming season.

Silver in the Moonlight

Dean's gaze traveled the length of her body and back up. "You look beautiful, as always."

Many men had called her beautiful before. It was an easily spoken compliment, one that usually didn't mean a whole lot to her. But something in the way Dean said it made her heart flutter and a flush sweep up her cheeks. Dean had meant it. He thought she was beautiful! The "as always" part was the kicker. Dean had seen her only in jeans, shorts, and assorted tops and he still thought she was beautiful. He had seen her before she had had her first morning cup of coffee, and still he thought she was beautiful. She couldn't meet his eyes, so she looked at his shoes. "Thank you."

His finger was warm against her chin as he tilted her face up. "You're blushing."

She grimaced. He didn't have to sound so damn pleased with that observation. "I am not." She jerked her chin out of his grasp. "Are you ready to go?"

"I've been counting the minutes since we parted this morning." He fell in step beside her as she started back across the driveway. As she headed toward the garage his hand shot out and he grabbed her elbow. "You're not planning on taking the boat, are you?"

"It's a Buick, not a boat." At least she wasn't the only one who considered the classic an eyeful as well as a roadful. "It's either the Buick or Sadie and Ida get to sit on your lap."

He chuckled. "They're the wrong Silver." His grin was wicked and she knew what he had meant, but she didn't respond. "There is one more suggestion."

"What's that?" she asked politely. She couldn't get the image of her sitting on his lap out of her mind.

"I'll drive." He nudged her in the direction of the house. "Go get your aunts while I get my car."

She wasn't about to look a gift horse in the mouth. Her arms were sore from pulling miles of jasmine off the house. She couldn't even begin to guess how many turns there were to Lucinda's. "Thanks, Dean. I really appreciate it."

He gave her such a soft look, it melted the fringes of her heart. "It's my pleasure, Katherine."

She practically floated back to the house to get her aunts.

Dean smiled at his dinner partners. The three beautiful women had been attracting quite a lot of attention in the past hour, especially Katherine. But Sadie and Ida had been receiving their fair share from some of the older refined gentlemen in the restaurant. The amazing part was, all three ladies didn't seem to notice.

More than that was amazing, Dean thought as he tuned back into the conversation. Sadie and

Silver in the Moonlight

Ida were actually listening to Katherine and agreeing to allow their house to be inspected. Not that he believed they would agree to any of the work that needed to be done, but it was a start. Katherine had accomplished in three days what he and the town had failed to do in fifteen months.

"Sadie, Ida," she was saying now, "do you know of anyone who recently had their house restored or repaired?"

"Everyone in town is having something done," Ida grumbled. "Bart and Lillian just had one of those fancy sunrooms put on."

Dean couldn't fathom it. Ida sounded jealous of Bart and Lillian's remodeling. But why? Ida had been fighting just as hard as Sadie not to have anyone look at their house. It wasn't because they couldn't afford to restore the entire place to its original beauty. Between what their father had left them and what their brother's estate had added to that, they could buy the whole town, possibly even twice. He should know. Sadie and Ida were his bank's wealthiest clients.

"Did you like the way the room turned out, Ida?" he asked.

"It's on the small side, but it seems comfortable enough," Ida grudgingly admitted.

"It has a lovely view of Sherman's Creek," Sadie added.

"Do you know the name of the contractor

who did the work?" Katherine asked. "We could ask them to inspect your place."

"I could ask Lillian," Sadie said.

Katherine glanced at Ida. "She must have been so jealous all these years."

"Of what?" questioned Ida.

"Why, of Sadie's and your sunroom, of course." Katherine smiled at her aunts. "You two have had that gorgeous sunroom since you were learning your ABCs. Sherman's Creek is okay to look at, but it's nothing compared to the river."

Sadie beamed. "True."

Ida took longer to answer. "I do like our view better." She toyed with her water glass, but didn't pick it up. "Maybe we can ask this contractor how much he would charge to paint our sunroom."

"A cheery yellow," Sadie said.

"Or a light blue," Ida said. "The color of the morning sky on a clear June day."

Dean glanced at Katherine, met her gaze, and grinned. The Silver sisters were hooked. He wasn't worried about what color they wanted the sunroom painted. He was more concerned that the glass room, which ran practically the entire length of the back of their house, be safe.

"Well, ladies," he said, "who's ready for dessert?"

Half an hour later Dean pulled into Sadie and Ida's driveway and parked directly behind Katherine's red sports car. "Here we are, ladies. Home safe and sound."

"Thank you, Dean. Dinner was wonderful," Sadie said.

"I can't remember when I ate so much," Ida said. "Thank you, Dean."

"You're both welcome. It was my pleasure." He glanced at Katherine sitting beside him in the front seat. She was still miffed at him because he'd refused to allow her to pick up the check. He knew this was the nineties and equality was now firmly entrenched in every modern-day male, but he couldn't ignore his upbringing or his grandfather's lessons of how a man should treat a lady.

He got out of the car and helped Sadie exit the rear seat. Katherine got out of the front seat and was helping Ida before he could make it around to that side of the car. She gave him a look that clearly said she wasn't done voicing her objections to the way he had handled the check back at Lucinda's.

Ida and Sadie climbed the two steps to the front porch. Katherine hung back with him by the car. He wasn't looking forward to the ensuing argument with her. He would much rather end their evening on friendlier terms.

"Are you coming, Katherine?" Ida asked.

"Oh, hush, Ida. Leave them be," Sadie whispered loudly enough for them both to hear.

"They're young, the night's still young, and the moon is simply gorgeous tonight."

Ida said something he couldn't hear, but again Sadie's voice came clear and bright. "You two go take a stroll in the moonlight or something equally romantic. We old biddies need our rest so we can dream about our own misspent youth."

Dean chuckled. He liked Sadie's way of thinking. "I'll take good care of your niece."

"Neither one of you is an old biddy," Katherine said.

"Good night," Ida called.

"Good night," Sadie added. "We'll leave the door unlocked for you, Kitty."

"I won't be long," Katherine said, sending Dean an inscrutable look. "Good night, you two. And sleep tight, because first thing tomorrow morning I want to hear all about your 'misspent youth.'"

Ida muttered something and Sadie giggled like a schoolgirl as they entered the house.

Dean opened the passenger door of his car. "Are you up for a ride?" He had to distract her, and he knew the perfect way.

"A ride? At this hour of the night?" Katherine didn't step one foot closer to the car.

"You're not up to a little ghost watching?"

"Ghost watching?"

He knew he had her by the expression on her face. Even in the dim porch light he could see her curiosity. "Molly's ghost." He shrugged as if it

Silver in the Moonlight

didn't make any difference to him. "I thought you might be interested in driving up to Molly's Park and seeing for yourself."

She stepped closer to the door. "I thought you didn't believe in ghosts."

"I don't." He forced himself not to smile. "But I've never been to Molly's Park after dark. I'm game for a little ghost watching if you are."

Katherine slipped into the car. "This doesn't mean that I've forgiven you for the sneaky way you disobeyed me at the restaurant."

His gaze followed the shimmery silkiness of her legs as she swung them into the car. Lord, her legs were enough to drive a priest to sin. Thank goodness he wasn't a priest. He closed her door, walked around the front of the car, and climbed in behind the wheel. "I'm sorry I took care of the check while you and Ida were in the ladies' room. It was a sneaky thing for me to do, but you're fighting over one hundred and fifty years of Southern manners that have been inbred within my genes."

"Only one hundred and fifty years?" Katherine looked mighty pleased with herself. "The Silvers go back over two hundred years."

Dean started the car and backed out of the driveway. "For a Yankee you sure do have your share of Southern pride."

"I happen to have been born in Charleston."

"So was I, and there I stayed." He drove in

the direction of Molly's Park. "Why did your family move to Boston?"

"I don't know." She glanced out the side window. "That's not right. I do know why we moved to Boston, but I don't know what happened to split the family." A heavy sigh escaped her lips. "My father met and fell in love with Elizabeth Roland while she was visiting Charleston. Within a year they were married, and had bought a house near my grandfather's warehouses, where my father was being groomed to take over the business."

"What type of business?"

"Importing and exporting. Charleston, as you know, is a major seaport on the East Coast. A lot of things are needed to be shipped out, and a lot are shipped in. From what I understand, my grandfather owned the majority of warehouses on the Ashley River side of Charleston, and quite a few on the Cooper River side."

"I'm impressed." He wasn't only impressed, he was in awe. Now he understood where Sadie and Ida got all their money. Katherine's grandfather had been filthy rich.

"Well, obviously my father wasn't. My mother's father owned the Roland Shipyards in Boston. A couple of years after they were married and I was born, my grandfather in Boston became ill. He needed help to run the shipyard and his first choice was his son-in-law, my father."

"So your father left Charleston for Boston."

"Yes, but the move severed all ties with his father and his aunts. I'm not sure why. All I know is my father refuses to discuss his Southern roots, or even acknowledge his aunts."

"He must have hurt his father pretty badly when he turned his back on the family business to help run a Boston shipyard." He understood the Southern tradition of sons following in their fathers' footsteps. His own father had expected him to be a banker since the day Dean was born, and he had never thought or dreamed of being anything else. He didn't know what his father would have done if he had defied the Katz tradition and taken up a different profession.

"Okay," Katherine said, "I can see where some hurt and disappointment enter into the picture, but not enough to never talk to one another again." She turned and looked at him. "What about Sadie and Ida? From what I've heard, they adored my father the whole time he was growing up. They accepted my mother into the family, and they spoiled me rotten the first four years of my life. Even after we moved away they continued to send me a Christmas and birthday present every year."

"Sadie and Ida would stand behind any decision their brother made, Katherine."

"Why?"

"Sadie and Ida are from the old school. They were provided for, protected, and loved by the Silver men. Their father gave them everything they could ever want or need. Since neither one married, Hamilton took over that responsibility when their father died. It would be completely natural for them to stand with Hamilton on whatever decision he made concerning your father. I know it sounds barbaric, but Sadie and Ida only did what they had been taught to do—defer to the men of the family."

"It sounds worse than barbaric, it sounds asinine."

Dean reached over and covered one of her fists with his hand. "Did your paternal grandfather ever send you a Christmas or birthday present?"

"No."

He squeezed her hand. "Relax, Kate. Your aunts aren't as submissive as you seem to think."

"No?"

"No." He turned her hand over and laced his fingers with hers. "Hamilton never would have approved of them still communicating with you after your father moved to Boston. They defied him every time they sent you a present. Knowing Sadie and Ida, I bet they told him every time they sent you something. They don't like deceit or lies and could never live with the guilt of going behind Hamilton's back."

He had to release her hand as he pulled into Molly's Park. The paved road was narrow, and twisted and turned its way through the grove of old oaks. There were no streetlights in the park.

Silver in the Moonlight

There was no need for them. No one was supposed to be there after dusk.

The original deed of the forty-acre park specifically requested that it stay just as it was, just as Molly had loved it. Horse trails crisscrossed the park. Ancient oaks with bearded moss were everywhere. Children from town still splashed through the calf-high creek searching for crayfish and tadpoles on hot summer days. Molly would have loved it. If half the town's people were to be believed, Molly still loved it.

He drove slowly until he reached the place that was supposed to be Molly and her lover's rendezvous spot. He pulled the car onto a paved area and killed the engine. "This is it."

Katherine gazed out the windshield at the huge oak tree directly in front of them. "This is where Molly waits for her lover to return?"

"So the legend goes." He slid his arm along the back of the seat and toyed with her hair. He felt the slight tremor that went through her. "Scared?"

"No." She turned her head and smiled. "Don't you know that it's not the dead you have to fear, but the living?"

"So I've heard." He glanced at the massive old oak tree silhouetted against the night sky. "See, no Molly. So, what do you want to do now?" He could think of quite a few things he wouldn't mind doing with Kate right then.

"I thought Molly only appears on rainy nights."

She would have to remember that piece of information, he thought. "So far everyone who claims to have seen her says it was on a rainy night, but that doesn't mean she doesn't appear on clear nights too."

"You want to be the first to see her on a starry night?"

He wasn't positive, but there seemed to be a hint of laughter in her voice. "I don't want, or expect, to see her at all." He moved closer and wrapped a silky lock of her hair around his finger. "The reason everyone claims to see Molly's ghost on rainy nights is because they're probably seeing a hunk of wet moss hanging from the tree and blowing in the wind. Their overactive imaginations or the beer they shouldn't have been drinking supplies the rest."

"So you're saying Ida didn't see Molly's ghost?"

He hid his smile as she moved a couple of inches closer to him. "She probably saw something moving beneath the tree and concluded it was Molly."

"Don't you think Ida, or the rest of the people from town, are used to seeing moss hanging from trees?"

He released the curl and trailed his finger over her shoulder. The sweet fragrance of her perfume teased his senses and made him hunger

Silver in the Moonlight

to find the areas on her skin where she had dabbed the scent. "Sure they are, but they also were raised with the legend of Molly still haunting the area around that tree."

"So, instead of seeing moss, they see a ghost." She shook her head as she peered more closely at the tree.

"It's logical."

She turned her head to look at him. "Logic should have no place in such a tragic love story."

"You're a romantic." He already knew that, but he liked having it confirmed.

"There's nothing wrong with believing in love and happy endings." An enticing little frown pulled at the corner of her mouth. "Molly should have had a happy ending."

"Yes, she should have, but we can't change the past." He cupped her cheek and stroked her lower lip with his thumb. He'd been thinking about kissing her since he saw her standing in front of Ida's rosebushes that evening. Katherine was the beauty among the thorns.

That morning over breakfast he had tried everything to keep their meeting light, friendly, and neighborly. His hormones had been zinging through his body on overdrive. The treacherous little demons had remembered every sizzling moment of the night before when he and Kate practically made love on the riverbank. His dreams had been pure torture, and even the three-mile jog he'd taken that morning hadn't eased the throbbing strain. The cold shower he'd suffered through had been a total waste. As soon as he'd walked into his kitchen and seen Kate, he was once more aroused. The woman had done nothing but wrap her lips around the edge of his coffee cup and he ended up hard and throbbing.

It had taken every ounce of self-control he possessed not to pull her down onto the kitchen floor and plunge into her heat until the ache went away. He figured the stock market would hit three new record highs before they would be able to leave the house.

Kate's warm breath feathered across his thumb. "Are you going to kiss me, or do I have to beg?"

"If you beg, I'm a goner." Just thinking about her begging was enough to make him insane. He bent his head, captured her willing mouth, and fell into heaven.

Delicate fingers caressed his neck and pulled him closer. His tie was choking him and the suit jacket was sweltering, but he didn't care. He was kissing Kate.

She greedily kissed him back with a burning sense of frustration that matched his own. How was it possible for Kate to want him as much as he wanted her? The need to make love to her was burned into his soul. He had to make love to her or his life would have no meaning. After thirty-four years of living, he unexpectedly found the

Silver in the Moonlight

reason why he'd been put on this earth. He had been born to love Katherine Silver.

Kate nipped at his lower lip and he couldn't prevent the low groan of desire that vibrated through his chest. She caressed the front of his shirt, pressing her hand against his thundering heart. When she twisted deeper into his embrace he cursed the confines of the front seat of his car. He'd be damned if the first time he made love to Kate would be in his car in the middle of Molly's Park, where anyone could happen upon them.

He released her mouth and brushed a dozen kisses over her face and her moist lips. She tried to recapture his mouth, and though it took all his strength, he uttered the words he needed to say, but didn't want to. "We have to stop, Kate."

It took her a while before she asked, "Why?"

He sighed in frustration and kissed her brow. He didn't dare kiss her mouth again because he knew he wouldn't have the strength to stop a second time. "The police patrol the park constantly, Kate." He moved away from her and loosened his tie.

"Looking for Molly?"

"No, looking for teenagers necking in their cars." His fingers were trembling as he undid the top two buttons on his shirt.

He watched as Kate slid over to her side of the seat and tugged the hem of her dress back down over her shapely thighs. He swallowed hard.

Her smile pulled at his heart. "I don't think teenagers are the only ones necking in Molly's Park."

He reached out and tucked a golden curl behind her ear. "I do believe you're right." She pressed her warm cheek into his palm. "I don't know about you, but I'm getting too old to be caught necking in the front seat of my car."

"The last time I was caught necking in a car, it wasn't even my date's car. It was his father's."

He chuckled at the sound of disgust and embarrassment in her voice. "Come on, trouble. It's time I got you home before Sadie and Ida start to worry." He straightened behind the wheel and started the engine. "And just for the record, I've never been caught necking in *any* car."

He had been caught doing a lot more than necking in his father's den with the daughter of the bank's wealthiest client. His father's bank. He wasn't about to repeat that mistake with the niece of his own bank's wealthiest clients. Katherine Silver was going to be courted, wined and dined, and in no way was he going to put her in any compromising position. Whatever was happening between them was special enough not to risk it all in some wagging-tongue scandal.

Kate tilted up her chin as if she were royalty and said, "You must have had a very deprived childhood."

He laughed nearly the whole way back home.

SIX

The next morning Katherine spent half an hour walking along Main Street checking out the various businesses that filled both sides of the surprisingly busy street. She was impressed. Jasper had a splendid array of shops. If she'd had more time before her appointment she would have stopped into quite a few of them. She made a mental note to take some time to browse through town. That morning, though, she had an eleven o'clock appointment with Sadie and Ida's minister, Reverend Frost.

She felt a little self-conscious questioning a reverend, but his was the only name Sadie or Ida had given her as being a member of the Revitalization of Jasper Committee. She had a list of questions for him and she hoped he had some answers.

She had passed Jasper National Bank earlier

and had been tempted to stop in to see if Dean was working. The sign on the door said they were open on Saturday until noon. She had missed her morning cup of coffee because she had overslept. It was all Dean's fault. After he had dropped her off the night before she had lain in bed for hours wondering if she was doomed to know nothing but frustration during her stay in Jasper. Something special was happening between them, but every time she thought they were getting closer to each other, he backpaddled faster than a canoeist about to go over a waterfall. She had a feeling there was a lot more to Dean than met the eye.

His intelligence, professionalism, and ambition weren't in question. A man didn't own his own bank at thirty-four without having an abundance of all three of those qualities. That he was gorgeous went without saying, but Dean was also charming, nice, and courteous. All of that was admirable, but she needed to know more. Twice now, she would have willingly made love with the man in the most public of places, if he hadn't called a halt. Dean kissed her, and *bam*, she lost all her ability to think clearly. It was a new situation for her to be in, one she wasn't sure she liked. Dean not only had the power to make her lose control, he had the power to hurt her. It was a sobering thought. She didn't want to be hurt again.

She entered the Jasper Methodist Church

Silver in the Moonlight

through the side door, walked down a narrow hallway, and found Reverend Frost sitting behind a massive oak desk totally engrossed in whatever he was writing. She raised a hand and lightly tapped on the doorjamb.

Reverend Frost raised his head, immediately stood up, and came around from behind the desk. "Come in, come in. You must be Sadie and Ida's niece, Katherine."

She stepped into the room and shook his outstretched hand, returning his smile. Reverend Frost had snowy-white hair, a full beard, and twinkling blue eyes. Calling him stout would have been kind. In a red suit and driving a sleigh pulled by eight reindeers, Reverend Frost could have passed for Santa. The children of Jasper must love him. "And you must be Reverend Frost."

"The one and only." He waved his hand at an empty wing chair in front of his desk. "Please sit and tell me what this is all about. You said on the phone earlier that it was a matter of some importance. I hope Sadie and Ida are well."

"They're fine, Reverend Frost." She sat down and nervously straightened the arm covers on the chair. How did one confront a minister who looked like Santa and demand to know if he was trying to run her aunts out of their house?

"Call me Christopher or Chris." The reverend sat back down behind the desk. "Now, what's on your mind?"

"It's about the Revitalization of Jasper Committee. I understand you're on the committee."

"That's correct. I've been on it for about six months now."

She tried to think of a nicer way to phrase the question she needed to ask, but couldn't. Sometimes the truth needed to be plain and straightforward. "My aunts are under the impression that the committee is trying to get them to move out of their house and into the River View Rest Home. I was wondering if this possibly was true?" She silently congratulated herself on how calm and reasonable she sounded.

Reverend Frost blinked rapidly as a tide of red swept up his chubby face. "Oh my, no. Absolutely not. The committee would never force anyone from their home."

"I agree, the committee can't force my aunts to sell their house." The jolly reverend seemed to be hiding something. Why else would he be blushing like a bride on her wedding night? "I am curious to know if the committee is applying any type of pressure in that area, though." She crossed her legs and bounced the top foot up and down. Anyone who knew her well knew the bouncing foot was a sure sign she was thinking. Thinking hard and fast. Her father had once declared the bouncing foot meant trouble was brewing.

"Goodness, no. The committee was formed to revitalize the town and make it more appealing

Silver in the Moonlight

to tourists, not throw our good citizens out of their homes." The reverend reached into his pants pocket and pulled out a white cotton handkerchief and wiped at his brow. "Sadie and Ida are very dear to this town and to this church, Katherine. They have many friends and are well loved. Why, our altar would look mighty bare most of the year without Ida's lovely flowers. And no one can make a peach pie as delicious as Sadie."

"I know my aunts can cook and garden with the best of them, Reverend. What I want to know is how, or more accurately who, gave them the impression the committee wants them out of their beloved home?"

"I—I—I really can't say, Katherine. As far as I know, no one has approached them with the suggestion they pack their bags and head for River View." The reverend sadly shook his head. "The committee would never do such a low and cowardly thing. Dean wouldn't approve."

The bouncing foot stopped in mid-bounce, along with her heart. "Dean?"

"Dean Katz. He's the owner of Jasper's bank and he's your aunts' next-door neighbor. Haven't you met yet?"

"I know who Dean is, Reverend. What I don't understand is how he fits into all of this." Her mind was spinning in a dozen different directions.

"Dean's the one who formed the committee a

little over a year ago. It was his brainchild and the entire town is in his debt. If it weren't for him, Jasper would still be dwindling away to near extinction. Did you know that we were losing an average of three families a month before Dean stepped in?"

She barely listened as the reverend went on to list and exclaim over every one of Dean's accomplishments. The way the man was gushing on about Dean, she wouldn't be surprised to see a statue erected in the town square to honor him. Personally, she didn't care.

Only one thing was important. Dean had lied, or to be more accurate, he had omitted the truth. When she had questioned him about the committee the other morning, he had changed the subject. She had assumed he didn't know anything about it. How many times had her grandfather told her never to assume a damn thing in life? He used to chuckle and tell her it would turn around and bite her on the "assume." Well, her "assume" was mighty sore right now.

Dean had formed the committee. Dean had written her and suggested her aunts would be happier, and safer, in River View. Dean, with his hot sweet kisses, had betrayed her and her aunts. The man was lower than pond scum. And he was about to learn what it meant to mess with the Silvers.

Katherine abruptly stood and reached across

Silver in the Moonlight

the desk to shake the reverend's hand. "Thanks, Reverend Frost. You've been a great help."

Reverend Frost snapped his mouth closed in the middle of whatever compliment he was paying Dean and bewilderedly shook her hand. "Ah, it's been my pleasure, Katherine, and call me Christopher."

She pumped his hand and gave him a smile that strained her mouth. "Thanks again, Christopher."

"You're welcome. Give Sadie and Ida my best, and I hope to see the three of you at services tomorrow morning."

She absently nodded and headed for the door. The reverend's next words halted her in her tracks, though. "In case you're interested, the committee is meeting tomorrow night at seven. People from town and the surrounding community are invited and encouraged to attend the meetings. Seeing as you're Sadie and Ida's niece, I'm sure you'll be welcomed."

Oh, she wouldn't miss it for the world. "Where's the meeting held?"

"Here, in the basement. We have a fellowship hall down there with plenty of room for everyone." Christopher seemed quite pleased that she was considering coming.

"If I'm available I just might stop in. Thanks again."

She walked through the church and squinted at the bombardment of bright sunlight as she pushed open the side door and stepped outside. She might be available, but then again there was a chance she might not be. At this particular moment there was a real good chance she was about to be arrested for murdering a certain banker.

Her sneakers slapped at the pavement as she headed back toward her aunts' house. Temptation stood in her way, however. The Jasper National Bank. Without slowing her step, she pulled open the glass door of Dean's domain and stepped inside. It took her a matter of seconds to spot his office. As banks went, it was small. Three tellers, a drive-through window, and one lone secretary, off to the side, guarding Dean's office.

She headed for the secretary.

The pleasant-looking woman looked up. "Hello, how may I help you?"

"I need to see Dean."

"Do you have an appointment with Mr. Katz?"

"No, but he'll see me." She walked past the secretary's desk, heading for Dean's open door.

The secretary tried to block her way, but Katherine was quicker. She stepped into Dean's office just as his secretary reached his door. "Mr. Katz. I'm sorry, sir . . ."

Dean glanced up and smiled. "Kate, what a wonderful surprise." His smile slipped when he noticed she wasn't returning it. He glanced at the woman behind her. "It's okay, Shelia. This is

Silver in the Moonlight

Katherine Silver, Sadie and Ida Silver's niece. She's from Boston."

Katherine didn't like the way he mentioned where she was from. As if that explained why she had barged into his office.

"Hello, Ms. Silver." Shelia gave her a curious look before backing out of the doorway. "I'll just leave you two to discuss your business."

The door softly closed before Katherine could even offer the poor woman an apology.

Dean walked around his desk and approached her. "Kate, you seem upset. Is something wrong? Are Sadie and Ida all right?"

She turned and glared at him. Her finger shook as she pointed it at his chest. Dean stopped. "Don't you dare act as if you're concerned about my aunts."

"What are—"

"The game is up, Katz. I just found out about your precious committee."

"It's not my committee, Kate."

At least he wasn't denying knowing about the committee. "You didn't establish it?"

"Yes, I established it about fifteen months ago. I'm no longer on it, though."

"Did you or did you not know about the committee wanting to put Sadie and Ida into the same rest home as you mentioned in your letter to me."

Dean looked sad and tired as he leaned

against his desk. "The committee doesn't want that, Kate."

"Then who does?"

"There are a few, let's call them enthusiasts, in town who would like to see your aunts' place made into a bed-and-breakfast. The older, more historic homes have the greatest potential in that area. These 'enthusiasts' aren't on the committee, nor will they ever be, but they have the right to speak at the meetings, just like any other citizen."

"These enthusiasts have the right to terrorize my aunts while you and your committee do nothing about it?" She had thought Dean liked her aunts. He was going to be her shoulder to lean on when Sadie and Ida put up too much of a fuss about the repairs on their home. She had trusted him, and he had broken that trust. Whatever feelings she had started to develop toward him were crushed under the weight of his betrayal. He had known about this all along.

He pushed away from the desk. "No one is terrorizing your aunts, Kate."

She refused to meet his gaze. Tears were forming in her eyes, and she didn't want him to see that sign of weakness. Grandfather Roland would never have approved. "Tell that to those sweet old ladies who bake you chocolate-chip cookies and bring you vases filled with fresh-cut flowers. Tell it to them as they're wringing their wrinkled hands in distress and dabbing at tears with lace handkerchiefs." She gave Dean a look

Silver in the Moonlight

of pure loathing. "I hope you and your precious committee are proud of yourselves. You made two of the dearest, sweetest ladies God ever put on this earth afraid. They're afraid of what tomorrow might bring."

She walked out of his office and closed the door behind her. She heard Dean call her name twice, but she didn't stop. The tears she had been holding back were rolling down her cheeks. She didn't even stop to apologize for her earlier rudeness to the stunned-looking Shelia. She didn't stop until she was safely hidden behind a massive oak tree a few feet from the river's edge in Sadie and Ida's backyard.

Sometimes a person just had to get all the tears out of her system before she could again take up the battle.

Sunday evening at precisely seven o'clock Dean entered the church's basement with a sense of disillusion. His committee had failed. He had started it with a spark of an idea and a noble purpose. He had nurtured it for nearly a year, taught it right from wrong, and watched it grow. Like a loving parent, he had then backed away and allowed it to strive on its own. He wanted to bask in its accomplishments. Instead he was filled with a sense of shame for what he had created.

Kate had made him acknowledge that shame. After she had left the bank the previous morning he had gone in search of her, but couldn't find her. Sadie and Ida hadn't seen her. By evening, she had returned, but wasn't receiving visitors. Sadie and Ida were both duly concerned for their beloved niece. He had spent three hours in his backyard waiting to see if she would walk by the river once again. She hadn't.

That morning he had put on a large pot of coffee and fooled himself into thinking she would come. She hadn't.

He'd spent the entire afternoon reviewing what the committee had been doing without him at the helm. He should have attended more of the monthly meetings. Instead he had wanted the committee to stand on its own and had foolishly convinced himself that it was. The committee had been spending its time and energy bickering with a handful of zealous townfolks who only saw the mighty green dollar at the end of every decision. It was time for the bickering to stop.

He slid into the fellowship hall just as the meeting was being called to order. Taking a seat in the back of the room, he glanced around. The six members of the committee were familiar to him, as was the majority of the audience. His heart skipped two beats when he noticed Kate sitting in the second row. He'd figured she would be there. He'd also figured Sadie and Ida wouldn't be. Kate wouldn't allow them to witness this mockery of a once-noble cause.

He studied the proud tilt of Kate's chin as the

Silver in the Moonlight

committee reported the "Good News" part of the meeting. There were relatively few pieces of good news. The "New Business" portion of the meeting was short as well and sadly lacking in anything substantial. Dean's heart sank a little deeper. He'd known the revitalization of Jasper would slow down after the initial takeoff, but this was depressing. Why hadn't he bothered to attend one of these meetings in the last four months?

Because he had had faith in his concept. Jasper needed to be revitalized by the citizens of Jasper, not the new banker in town. He hadn't wanted one person to take the credit for the resurrection of the town. He'd wanted the whole town to be proud of their accomplishments.

The business portion of the meeting came to a close and Reverend Frost opened the meeting to the floor so the citizens could express their concerns.

Beau Woodrow was the first to stand and voice his opinion. Beau was one of the enthusiasts Dean had told Kate about and he tended to voice his opinions loudly, often, and usually with all the finesse of a fox in a henhouse. The first words out of his mouth caused Dean to shudder. "We need more places for the tourists to stay. They're plopping down some big bucks to stay in old houses with character."

"Beau," said one of the men on the committee, "we've already gone over this. Anyone who was interested in opening their home as a bed-and-breakfast has been offered the opportunity to do so. Jasper has only a limited supply of historic homes and many of the owners wish those homes to remain private."

"What about the old Albert place? The house has been empty for three months now."

"Stewart Albert willed the house to his grandson, who lives in California. We contacted the grandson to see if he was interested in selling and were informed he wished to keep the house as a summer home for his family."

"What about the Burleigh place or the Silver place? Both homes are falling into disrepair. They're eyesores. Hell, you can barely see the Silver place for all the damn flowers and trees."

"Mr. Woodrow," Reverend Frost snapped. "I wish to inform you this is a public town meeting and that Sadie and Ida Silver's niece, Miss Katherine Silver, is present." The reverend nodded in Kate's direction and offered her an apologetic smile.

Kate stood and gave Beau Woodrow a look that made the hair on the back of Dean's neck stand straight up. She looked ready to rip the poor man's jugular from his throat, not that he blamed her. Beau Woodrow was an ass.

"Mr. Woodrow, you and the rest of this town should be ashamed of yourselves." Kate glared at the audience before turning her attention to the committee members sitting at a table in the front

Silver in the Moonlight

of the room. "Who gave this committee or this town the right to terrorize your older citizens?"

"This committee doesn't condone terrorism to any of our citizens, Katherine." Reverend Frost looked both angry and embarrassed.

"You all condone it by allowing jerks like Woodrow here to speak openly and freely." She jerked her thumb in Beau's direction, but didn't bother to look at him. "What he says gets back to those he offends, and they believe the committee has sanctioned his every word. My aunts are now living in fear that someone is going to take their house and pack them off to the River View Rest Home."

Dean heard the gasps of outrage throughout the crowd. Every one of them seemed to pierce his heart.

"My aunts will not be going to River View or any other rest home, Mr. Woodrow. Sadie was born in that house, and that is where she wants to stay. Ida might have been born in the family's Charleston house, but her heart has always been in Jasper." Kate took a deep breath and squared her shoulders as she faced Beau Woodrow. "You will not be dealing with my two elderly aunts any longer. You will be dealing with me, and I don't scare so easily."

"Miss Silver," Reverend Frost called over the thunderous applause. "I'm sure Dean Katz would agree with me when I say we are truly sorry for any worries or fears we might have inadvertently caused your aunts."

Dean had heard and seen enough. Woodrow was still the arrogant ass he always had been, the committee had lost its backbone to control such idiots, and Kate was magnificent. He stood up and walked to the front of the room. "Dean Katz can and will speak for himself." He heard people murmuring and knew the majority of the audience hadn't known he had been sitting in the back of the room. Kate had known he was there. She had looked everywhere, but in his direction.

He nodded at the committee, then turned and faced the audience. Both Kate and Woodrow had retaken their seats. "I believe it's my turn to speak." He looked at Kate and offered her a small smile. "Miss Silver, I'll make my own apologies to Sadie and Ida later, but for now I wish to say that I am sorry you've been dragged into this mess, but I appreciate your willingness to bring it to my attention." Poor Shelia would never get over seeing a woman running from his office crying. She had glared daggers at him until they'd locked the doors of the bank at noon the day before.

"Jasper is a good town, with more than its fair share of fine upstanding citizens. I hope you will give us a chance to show you how generous and kind we can be." He took a deep breath and met the gaze of a dozen or so men and women from the audience whom he knew. They were business

Silver in the Moonlight

associates, customers at his bank, or just people he considered friends. Every one of them looked as upset as he felt.

"I heard about the few enthusiasts who were making some waves at these meetings, but I considered it a good sign. Smooth sailing usually means you're sailing on the easiest course, and not necessarily the right one. I thought a different point of view would be good for the soul. I was wrong.

"It never crossed my mind that disgruntled words would be taken for the truth and that people would be hurt, or worse, live in fear. But that is what happened. On my way here tonight I stopped at Edison Burleigh's place. He, too, has heard the rumors and is fearful of being shipped off to River View. I assured him this would not happen, and I'm pretty sure he believed me. But I don't feel any better, and neither should this town. This committee was set up to improve Jasper. Instead we have caused fear in our own most valued citizens. Edison, Sadie, and Ida have given this town so much over the years, and this is how we repay them? By making them fear for their future!

"I founded this committee to reach for a noble cause, to save a town. The cause is no longer noble. I think it's time that the Revitalization of Jasper Committee be disbanded."

He could feel Kate's gaze follow him as he exited the room. His footsteps on the tiled floor was the only sound. He had one more stop to make that night before heading home. Sadie and Ida deserved his apology and his reassurances.

As for Kate, he didn't know what to do about her. He understood her anger and how the whole situation must appear to her. He had not only formed the committee that was currently terrifying her aunts, but he had written to her and suggested the River View Rest Home as a possible option for Sadie and Ida. Two strikes against him, but he wasn't out yet. He needed time to step out of the batter's box and regroup.

By late Monday afternoon, Katherine couldn't stand to be cooped up in the house any longer. She needed air. Lots of air. Since seven o'clock in the morning she had been following Ralph Chesney around, obediently looking at whatever he pointed at, and cringing every time he tsked over a warped windowsill or an uneven floorboard. She didn't even want to think about his reaction to the roof or the basement. The man looked about as cheerful as a pallbearer at his best friend's funeral.

Ralph Chesney wasn't inspecting her aunts' beloved house and seeing dollar signs. He was inspecting her aunts' house and seeing a wonderful old home in need of many repairs. Ralph Chesney had love in his eyes as he inspected the sloping built-in mahogany bookcases in the front parlor and the ornamental ironwork surrounding the outside of the sunroom. Katherine had paid closer attention to his expression than to the problems he pointed out to her. Ralph Chesney would lovingly restore and repair her aunts' home.

As for the price he would charge, she didn't even want to think about it. Her head was already pounding with the mere possibilities of what the figure might be. To be honest with herself, her head was pounding more from lack of sleep than astronomical restoration bills.

Dean Katz had thrown her and the entire town a curveball the night before when he suggested that the committee be dissolved. She had sat there in stunned silence for a long time after he had walked out of the meeting. He hadn't acted like a man who wanted to push her aunts into some rest home and use their house to fill a need for another bed-and-breakfast.

He had acted like a man who hadn't realized what had been going on until it was too late. He had accepted the burden of guilt for what the committee had done inadvertently. He had cared enough to stop by Edison Burleigh's house and offer an old man the comfort of knowing no one was going to take his home away. Dean had also stopped in and had a talk with Sadie and Ida before she got home from the meeting. Her aunts had been grinning like two teenagers on their way to the prom when she walked through the door.

Everything should have been right in Jasper. Except it wasn't. The townfolks were in a panic as to what would happen if the committee was dissolved. Beau Woodrow had appeared quite embarrassed as he snuck out of the hall during the confusion that reigned after Dean's departure. Reverend Frost had been so dazed by the onslaught of questions that he called an end to the meeting and rescheduled it for next Sunday night, when things had had a chance to calm down.

She had sat quietly in her folding chair, wondering how she could have misjudged Dean so horribly. The only answer she could come up with arrived far into the night as she lay on a too soft mattress staring at her bedroom ceiling. She had expected Dean to betray her. It was that simple.

The only man in her life who had never deceived her had been her grandfather Roland. Every man back in Boston who had shown one ounce of interest in her had done so only because of the Silver fortune and the Roland Shipyard. Her own father had conspired with Todd Rutledge and was constantly pushing her in a direction she had no desire to take. Even her brother was against her and couldn't understand why she disagreed constantly with their parents.

She stepped off the back porch and onto a

garden path. Sadie and Ida were waiting for her at the white iron table and chairs tucked beneath a tree. She glanced over at Dean's house and wondered if he would accept her apology if she came bearing gifts, like a plate filled with Sadie's chocolate-chip cookies straight from the oven.

Sitting down with her aunts, she accepted the tall glass of lemonade Sadie handed her.

"Is *he* gone?" Sadie asked.

"Yes." She had to smile at the way both Sadie and Ida referred to Ralph Chesney. They had made themselves scarce during his inspection, but had insisted she accompany the contractor as he measured and examined every nook and cranny of the old house. "He said he won't have any kind of estimate till the end of the week."

"He didn't talk about changing anything, did he?" Ida asked.

"No. I told him exactly what you two told me. You didn't want any changes, just a repair here and there." She sipped her cool drink and frowned at the floating ice cubes crashing into each other. "I'm not sure how to approach this subject with either one of you, so I'm going to be blunt. The house is in pretty bad shape. Ralph did admit to me that it needs a lot of repairs, major repairs." She made sure both of her aunts were paying close attention before adding, "Very expensive repairs."

"Oh my." Sadie sighed.

"Dear me," added Ida.

Katherine pressed her fingers against the condensation coating the outside of her glass. "I don't want you two to worry about the money." She had absolutely no idea how well-off her aunts were. She knew they had been well taken care of by their father, and then their brother. But still, the cost to restore the house was going to surpass the fair-market value of the place as it stood. Grandfather Roland always told her to use her inheritance wisely and from the heart, and she knew he would have approved of what she was about to do. "I have a nice-sized nest egg sitting around collecting dust. Consider it yours."

"Oh my," cried Sadie.

"Oh dear," echoed Ida.

Katherine smiled. "You two already said that."

"We don't need your money, Kitty." Sadie looked appalled by the very idea.

"I know you don't need it, but I would like for you two to have it. The house needs major renovation before it crumbles into dust. I really would like to see it kept standing. Besides, I need a place to stay in Jasper when I come and visit you two."

"Really, Kitty, we don't need your money. We have more than enough."

"That's true," seconded Ida. "We couldn't spend it all if we had to."

Katherine figured that as long as Sadie had

Silver in the Moonlight

money to buy flour and eggs and Ida an occasional bulb or new seedlings, they probably would consider it enough. More money than one could spend in a lifetime. Wouldn't that be wonderful? "If you two have so much money, why hasn't anything been done to the house?"

"We don't want to spend your inheritance, Kitty."

Katherine frowned. Sadie and Ida were looking quite pleased with themselves. The sweet dears were finally showing signs of their age. "What are you talking about?"

"Sadie and I decided years ago to make you our heir." Ida smiled. "After we are gone, you get everything."

"The Silver fortune will be yours, dear." Sadie patted her hand. "We've had a good life, Kitty. We never wanted for anything. We want you to have that same luxury."

Katherine sat there in stunned silence.

"Papa always said it wasn't right for a woman to work outside of the home," Ida said. "We know things have changed and a lot of women like to do things, but we can't see how you can support yourself by sending people off on vacations."

"In our day," added Sadie, "a woman had her father and then a husband to support her." Sadie smiled at Ida. "We weren't blessed with husbands, but we had our brother to look after us."

"We want you to be taken care of after we're gone," Ida said.

Katherine felt tears well up in her eyes. "That's the nicest thing anyone has ever done for me." She reached out and took their hands in hers. "I'm truly touched, but I don't want your money." She gave them a watery smile. "In fact, I don't even need the Silver fortune. Grandfather Roland left me quite enough. If I decided tomorrow never to work again, I wouldn't starve."

"Oh my." Sadie sighed, sounding slightly disappointed.

"Oh dear," echoed Ida.

"I appreciate the thought, but I would rather you spend some of that Silver fortune on restoring the house. Not only will the house be worth a whole lot more, but if you two expect it to be standing for any future generations of Silvers, you have to do something about it now. In another decade or so it might not be fixable."

She could actually see the spark of interest ignite in her aunts' eyes. She didn't know what had caused it, the part about future generations of Silvers or the desire to see the house brought back to its former glory. Either way she'd take it. Sadie and Ida were hooked on the idea of restoring the house. She just hoped they wouldn't pass out at the sight of Ralph Chesney's estimate.

Sadie and Ida put their heads together and whispered back and forth. When they separated and looked at her, both wore a serious expression. "We would like to think it over," Ida said.

Katherine picked up her glass and hid her smile behind it. They were going to do it. "Sure, talk it over some, ask questions in town, and see the estimate before you commit."

SEVEN

Katherine switched the glass dish containing a hot cherry cobbler from one hand to the other as she made her way down the crushed-shell driveway and around the killer roses. Even with potholders, the heat was warming her hands a few degrees past the comfort stage. She could have waited longer before rushing over to Dean's, but she hadn't wanted to. She needed to talk to him before he did anything rash, like dissolve the committee.

When she had told her aunts she was planning on paying Dean a visit after dinner, Sadie had insisted she would bake "that dear sweet boy" a pie. Katherine had vetoed her aunt's suggestion, baking a cherry cobbler herself instead. Sadie had nervously paced the kitchen's worn linoleum and watched her every move as she mixed the ingredients. By the time she had slid the cob-

Silver in the Moonlight

bler into the oven, she had been as nervous as Sadie, even though she had made the very same cobbler dozens of times.

She had shooed her aunts out of the kitchen to go get ready for their customary Monday-night card game with a few of their friends. While the cobbler baked she had cleaned up the dinner dishes. Her aunts had reentered the kitchen the same moment she was pulling the cobbler from the oven. Sadie had beamed with pride and declared that Katherine possessed the Silver touch in the kitchen. Ida had argued that Katherine possessed the Silver touch in the gardens. Both of her aunts had left the house still arguing over which family traits their niece might have inherited. Katherine hadn't wanted to interrupt their good-natured argument by informing them that her mother was not only an avid gardener but a wonderful cook when she deemed it necessary to step into the kitchen.

She had only taken a few minutes to run a brush through her hair and to make sure she didn't have any flour dusting her face before picking up the cobbler and heading for Dean's. Earlier she had showered away the grime she had accumulated from the house inspection while Sadie prepared dinner.

She was almost to Dean's front steps before she noticed he was sitting on the porch. He looked like a man with a lot on his mind and the world upon his shoulders. He also looked like he was bending the long board he was sitting on. She set the hot cobbler on the wooden floor of the porch and slowly climbed the three steps.

She met Dean's inquiring gaze with a tentative smile. She couldn't blame him for being a bit leery. Their last two encounters hadn't been particularly pleasant. She needed a safe, neutral opening. "It's a beautiful evening tonight."

"Most evenings in Jasper are beautiful." Dean lightly bounced on the board.

She eyed the contraption he was sitting on and couldn't help asking what he was doing. She had noticed the long benchlike board on a couple of other porches.

"I'm joggling. It's great for soul-searching."

Juggling she understood, but joggling? The nearly black board was sixteen feet long and held at each end by braces with rockers on the bottom. Dean's weight at the center was causing the board to dip, and with a light motion of his feet he was bouncing, ever so gently. "What's joggling?"

He smiled. "You've never joggled?"

"Miss Snodgrass wouldn't have approved." She matched his smile and felt a weight lift off her shoulders. Everything was going to work out. Dean wasn't going to kick her and her cobbler off his porch.

He moved down to one end of the board and nodded to the other end. "Sit down and I'll teach you how to joggle. It's a fine Southern tradition."

Silver in the Moonlight

"Well, since it's a tradition." She sat down on the other end and felt the board dip under her weight. The tips of her sneakers barely touched the floor of the porch. As she bounced slightly she slid an inch closer to the center of the board.

"This is called a joggling board," Dean explained. "It's been around since the early 1800s. I believe the original design came from Scotland, but they became very popular on plantations and with the Low-Country residents."

Katherine could feel herself slipping ever closer to the center of the board as Dean continued his story.

"During the Civil War, General Beauregard did a lot of his soul-searching and military planning while joggling at his residence in Charleston."

"General Beauregard? Imagine that." She tried to appear properly impressed while hiding her smile. Dean was working his way down the board, too, and the conclusion was obvious. They were going to meet in the middle.

"Don't they have joggling boards in Boston?"

"Not that I've seen. We tend to do our soul-searching in rockers."

"Hmmm . . . That explains the Boston rocker." Only a foot of empty board remained between them. "There's an interesting legend about the joggling board."

"Does it contain a ghost?" She glanced at the remaining eight inches of board separating them.

Joggling definitely held some interesting possibilities.

"No." He grinned at her. "Legend has it that there was never an unmarried daughter at any home that had a joggling board."

Katherine's bare thigh brushed against Dean's. His shorts were longer than hers, but even through the cotton fabric she felt the softness of the dark golden hair that covered his legs. She smiled as his arm went around her and pulled her closer. They were hip to hip and thigh to thigh. "Are there any unmarried daughters living in this house?"

"Not a one."

She snuggled deeper into his embrace. "Damn thing must work, then."

He chuckled before lowering his head and capturing her mouth in a kiss guaranteed to set the aged joggling board on fire. Katherine melted under the heat of that kiss.

She opened her mouth to the demanding sweep of his tongue and wrapped her arms around his neck. Tongues danced in a rhythm as old as the tides. The blood rushing through her veins pulsed to the same rhythm. Desire flared at the apex of her thighs.

The last couple of days had seemed like an eternity without his warmth. Without his kisses. Some important light had been dimmed in her life, and she hadn't realized it until now, when his touch sparked it anew. Dean was the keeper of

Silver in the Moonlight

that flame, and she wanted to bask in its glow. She wanted to see how high the blaze would burn. She wanted to experience all of it. She wanted to make love with Dean.

She turned farther into his embrace and nearly fell off the board. Dean's arms saved her from landing on the floor and making a fool of herself.

He broke the kiss and steadied her. "I now see why plantation owners allowed their daughters to entertain suitors on the joggling board."

She clung to his arm as the board dipped and bounced. For two cents she would gladly burn the stupid thing. "There definitely wasn't a lot of hanky-panky going on while they bounced their way to nausea." She tried to settle the board and her stomach.

Dean laughed while he stood up and pulled her off the board. "I guess joggling takes some getting used to."

She wanted to tell him it wasn't so much the joggling that made her lose her balance, but his kisses. "Yeah, I guess it's my Northern upbringing."

He kissed the tip of her nose. "You do have the most adorable Yankee accent."

She frowned up at him, more because of the sisterly kiss on her nose than the comment about her accent. "My father would be mighty happy to hear that."

"I imagine he would." Dean nodded toward

the baking dish covered in aluminum foil sitting near the top step. "What did Sadie send over this time?" He looked more hopeful than resigned.

"Sadie didn't send anything."

"Ida baked?" He shook his head in amazement. "Ida usually stays out of Sadie's domain."

The toe of her sneaker tapped on the wooden floor of the porch. "It wasn't Ida, Dean. Guess again."

He turned his head and stared at her. "You baked?"

Her toe was no longer tapping, it was pummeling. "You don't have to sound so surprised. I do know how to cook."

"I didn't say you didn't." He bent down and carefully picked up the glass baking dish. "You're Sadie's niece, so I would assume you know how to do more in the kitchen than just boil water. But Sadie's usually very particular about who she allows in the kitchen. Last winter she caught the flu and still she barely allowed Ida to brew a pot of tea every once in a while."

"Sadie allowed me full range of the kitchen." She was quite pleased with that fact. "She even said I had the Silver touch when it came to baking."

Dean looked impressed. He carefully lifted the edge of the foil and sniffed. "Cherry cobbler! You baked cherry cobbler?"

She scowled. "No, I yanked it out of the grocer's freezer and plopped it into one of Sadie's baking dishes. How do you think that would have gone over with my aunt?" She had wanted to impress Dean with her cobbler, not astound him with the fact that she knew how to mix more than two ingredients in the same bowl.

"Sadie's heart would never have withstood the strain." He glanced hopefully at the dish in his hand. "Can we have some now so I can tell you how delicious it is?"

"On two conditions." It was hopeless, she decided. Dean would tell her it was delicious even if he had to wash it down with lubricating oil.

"Name them." He opened the front door and ushered her in.

"You supply the coffee and you must accept my apology."

He blinked and halted in the middle of the hall. "What apology?"

"The one I haven't had the chance to make yet."

"What do you have to apologize for?" He looked totally bewildered standing in his hall holding her peace offering.

"We can start with my barging into your office and yelling at you."

"You never yelled, Kate." He continued into the kitchen and set the warm dish on the counter. "I should be the one apologizing to you."

"You already did that quite nicely at the committee meeting last night." She jammed her hands into the pockets of her shorts and paced over to the screen door, glancing outside. Evening was approaching, but daylight hadn't lost the war yet. Her aunts' house looked run-down and shabby, the part she could see in between monster trees, shrubs, and climbing vines. Beau Woodrow had been right. It was becoming an eyesore.

She could hear Dean getting out the coffee and filters. The man was upholding his end of the bargain. Now all she had to do was find the right words. She had had them earlier, before she left her aunts'. Now they seemed to have deserted her.

She turned and watched as he poured in the water and flipped the switch. His white polo shirt and khaki shorts accentuated his tan beautifully. It was only the middle of spring and already his hair was streaked with blond highlights. She tried to imagine what he would look like come September and was utterly disarmed with the possibility. Dean Katz should have a line of women stretching from Jasper clean on up to Charleston. So why didn't he? What was his fatal flaw that she hadn't picked up on? Lord knows it had to be a whopper.

She leaned back against the doorjamb and blurted out the truth. "I have this problem with men."

Dean's hand froze in midair as he was reaching for the cups in the cabinet. He slowly turned and faced her. "What kind of problem?"

Silver in the Moonlight
139

What in the world had possessed her to say such a thing? It had to be all the attic dust she had inhaled while inspecting the leaking roof, or maybe it was the moist, moldy air in the basement. Either way, it must have rotted her brain. She could never remember saying something so damn stupid to a man before.

She shrugged and figured she didn't have any other option but to give Dean the truth. He deserved that much. "I don't trust them."

His gaze bore into her for a long time before he finally asked, "All men, or is it just me?"

"All men, except Grandfather Roland. He never once steered me wrong." She shifted her weight from foot to foot and waited for the look of disgust to darken his face. It didn't come.

"What about your father and brother?"

"My brother, the other Roland, follows in my father's footsteps so closely that sometimes it's hard to separate the two. As for my father, we never really had what one would call a 'close' relationship. He had expected some little girl who wore frilly dresses, gave tea parties, and took ballerina lessons. Instead he got me."

"I don't think he got such a bad deal." Dean pulled down the cups. "So what happened to sever the trust?"

"He arranged for me to marry Todd Rutledge."

"You're married?" Dean paled and looked as

shocked as if she had just told him she had been hatched from a gigantic pea pod.

"No, I've never been married." She shrugged and jammed her hands farther into her pockets. "Unbeknownst to me, my father knew the Rutledge family and Todd. He had thought Todd would make me a perfect husband, along with being the perfect son-in-law. I met Todd the week I moved home after graduating from college. I fell in love and by July we were engaged. By the end of August I found out that my father had arranged the whole thing and that Todd had only been interested in my share of my grandfather's inheritance." She could now tell the sad sordid story without feeling the heartbreak. She still felt the betrayal, but not the gut-wrenching pain of learning the man she had fallen in love with wasn't who she thought he was.

"He was a fool."

"Who? My father?" Edward Hamilton Silver would suffer a seizure if he ever heard anyone refer to him as a fool.

"Him, too, but I was referring to this Rutledge guy." Dean shook his head in wonder. "You fell in love with this guy, agreed to become his wife, and all he was after was whatever you'd inherited from your grandfather?" He ran his fingers through his hair and appeared to be on the verge of exploding. "What in the world did you inherit? Diamond mines in Africa? A Rembrandt collect? Half of Manhattan?"

Silver in the Moonlight

She smiled. Dean was doing wonderful things for her confidence. "No, nothing that impressive. Grandfather Roland left me one quarter of his shipyard."

Dean crossed the kitchen and cupped her face in his hands. His expression of anger had been replaced with comprehension. "Rutledge was a fool, Kate. Your love is worth more than a bunch of boats."

Katherine cringed. Grandfather Roland would surely roll over in his grave at someone referring to his ships as mere boats. "They're pretty imposing ships, Dean."

"They're nothing compared to you." He kissed the corner of her mouth. "Your apology is totally unnecessary, Kate. I realize what it must have looked like to you." He kissed the other corner of her mouth and then took a step back. "Why don't you dish out the cobbler while I pour the coffee?"

She wanted to apologize for not apologizing. She had handed Dean an excuse instead, a very bad excuse. He had recrossed the room and was busy pouring the coffee. She sighed and pulled the foil off the cobbler. Obviously food was more important to Dean than her apology.

She gave him a small smile as he joined her at the table and sat. "This looks delicious, Kate." She watched as he picked up a fork and sampled his first bite. He closed his eyes and slowly savored the cobbler.

"You can't do it, Dean."

His eyes flew open. "Do what?"

"Disband the committee."

"Are you referring to the committee I think you're referring to?"

She nodded. "The Revitalization of Jasper Committee." She reached for her cup and took a sip. "The town needs the committee, Dean."

"Why?"

"It's a good committee. A noble committee." She took a bite of her own cobbler. "I went to the meeting last night with the sole intention of trashing the committee members and the entire town, if need be."

"You had a very good reason to be upset, Kate. You saw what the rest of us blind fools didn't."

"No, what I saw was one bad element of the committee. I wasn't seeing the whole picture. Your committee has done some wonderful things for this town. Jasper is growing tremendously. This scare with Sadie and Ida was just a growing pain. It's worked out now, the pain has stopped." She reached out and covered his hand. "You don't have to eliminate the committee because of a few bad apples, Dean. Chuck the apples, or at least isolate them."

"Are you always so forgiving?"

"This has nothing to do with forgiveness. It's pure logic. You and the committee were doing what you thought was best." She ate more cob-

Silver in the Moonlight

bler, pleased that it had come out the way she intended. With Sadie glancing over her shoulder the entire time she was making it, she wouldn't have been surprised to find she'd left out an ingredient or two.

"Beau Woodrow did have a point," she went on, noticing that Dean had cleaned his plate. "My aunts' house is definitely leaning toward the "eyesore" category. The contractor came today to check it out. He'll have an estimate by the end of the week. My aunts and I had a nice chat and I'm pretty sure I've convinced them to stop saving their pennies for a rainy day." In reality, they had been saving them for *her* rainy days, not their own. She didn't want Dean to know that she had inadvertently been the reason her aunts' house was in the process of falling down around their heads.

"The committee shouldn't dictate how a person keeps their house, Kate."

"No, it shouldn't. But the committee is trying to sell the town, Dean. The whole town, especially the historic portion. Homes that are in that section should represent the best Jasper has to offer."

"What about the residents who can't afford to keep their homes in perfectly historical and well-maintained appearances? I don't want Jasper to turn into Charleston, where residents in the historic district have to get the neighborhood's approval on what color they want to paint their house."

"I'm not talking about taking it that far. What about if the committee tries to recruit some volunteers to help spruce up the homes of the residents who can't afford it, or who are physically incapable of fixing up their own homes?"

"Some of these old homes need a lot of work."

"I've been walking around the neighborhood, Dean. There's only one or two homes that look like they need major renovation, besides my aunts'."

Dean appeared to mull that one over. A minute later a smile teased the corner of his mouth. "I do believe you might have a pretty good idea there, Kate."

She raised one eyebrow and glared down her nose at him, giving him her best impersonation of a haughty snob. "What do you mean *might*?"

Dean's laughter filled the kitchen.

Three days later Katherine hurried down Main Street toward the bank. She was meeting Dean for lunch and she was going to be late. The boutique at the corner of Main and Lee had been too tempting to pass up. The gorgeous white sundress printed with sprigs of wisteria that had been displayed on the mannequin in the window was now safely nestled in the box in the shopping

Silver in the Moonlight

bag she was carrying. The floppy-brimmed straw hat that matched the dress perfectly was also in the bag, along with a bathing suit that was guaranteed to knock Dean's good intentions clean on their butt.

Over the past three days he had driven her to such a level of frustration, she was willing to use any method to seduce the man. For some reason she had yet to fathom, he refused to take the next step in their relationship and become her lover. He wanted to. That much was evident every night as he kissed her to near insanity. She could feel his desire. It matched her own.

So what was stopping him?

It was a good question. One she was bound and determined to find the answer to real soon. Something special was growing between them.

Katherine could see the bank, just three doors up on the opposite side of the street, when an empty shop caught her eye and halted her in the middle of the sidewalk. She had nearly passed it. She had been so intent on seeing Dean and daydreaming about when they would become lovers that she had nearly passed the empty shop with a discreet "For Rent" sign taped to the window.

She had no idea how she ended up with her nose pressed to the glass staring inside the small store, which was maybe fifteen feet by twenty feet. The walls and trim were painted a drab beige and the brown carpet appeared threadbare and worn. She pressed closer and blocked her eyes from the fierce glare of the sun.

It was perfect.

She hadn't even been aware of her dream until she stood there staring at it. She wanted to open her own travel agency and Jasper was the perfect place to do it. It was a growing town. The nearest travel agency was in Beaufort, ten miles away. Her aunts needed someone close by to keep an eye on them. The contractor could fix the house up, but who was going to make sure Ida didn't go wandering off in search of buried treasure, or that Sadie blew out all the candles?

Then there was Dean. Did she really want to go back home to Boston without discovering where all their passionate kisses were leading? Her heart was telling her she was falling in love, not only with Dean, but with the Southern charm of the town called Jasper.

She turned and studied the street. Townspeople as well as tourists, with cameras slung around their necks, strolled along the sidewalks. The little shop was in an ideal location. Jasper was still small enough that she could handle the office without the aid of a support staff or additional agents. She knew the business well, considering that she had been in it for five years. The prospect of being her own boss held a certain appeal. A certain remarkable appeal.

She turned back to the store and envisioned posters on the window picturing places like Paris

Silver in the Moonlight

in the spring, the Colosseum in Rome, San Francisco. The exterior door and window trim needed to be repainted. The inside definitely needed a new carpet and bright paint on the walls. She would put her desk in the back and arrange a few chairs about a coffee table toward the front. A set of shelves and a couple of file cabinets to hold the mountain of brochures. Some framed photographs of foreign cities and New York at night to decorate the walls. Her apartment in Boston held a treasure trove of decorating ideas that she had accumulated from her own travels; a Mardi Gras mask from New Orleans, a sombrero from Mexico, a bust of Queen Nefertiti from Egypt, seashells from the Caribbean, just to name a few. More than enough to decorate one simple office.

Katherine closed her eyes and clearly saw herself sitting in her new office. She smiled at the picture. If she believed in omens, she would definitely take this empty shop as one. She was meant to open her own travel agency. That was why she had been so dissatisfied in Boston. She had been working for someone else.

She hadn't proved to her father that she did possess the Silver initiative when it came to business. All she had done was prove she could manage to *live* on her own. It was time she proved she could *make* it on her own.

Everything she needed was right here in Jasper.

"See anything interesting?"

She jumped at the nearness of Dean's voice. She hadn't heard him come up behind her and stare in the window over her shoulder. She must have been later than she thought for their lunch date and he had come looking for her. She gave the empty shop one last glance before turning away and smiling up at Dean. "Only my future," she answered.

EIGHT

Katherine glanced over at Dean walking beside her, and smiled. She couldn't help but smile. She hadn't been able to wipe the silly smirk off her face all evening. One minute she had been sitting on the lawn of Jasper's Park listening to the sweet sounds of cool jazz being played for the town's Saturday-night entertainment, and the next she had turned to say something to Dean and it hit her. She was in love with him!

She twirled the floppy-brimmed straw hat clutched in her hand. She hadn't been able to resist wearing the dress she had bought the other morning, or its matching hat, to the festivities that night. She would much rather be holding Dean's hand than her hat, but Sadie and Ida were walking home directly in front of them. Ida would never approve of such a bold move.

Her dear sweet aunts were cramping her style.

Ida had spread their blanket directly next to hers and Dean's on the park lawn and no amount of persuading on Sadie's part could get her to move it. Ida had been hovering over her all evening long.

Dean returned her smile. "Did you enjoy yourself?"

"It was wonderful." She quickly brushed a kiss across his cheek as Sadie and Ida turned the corner onto Jackson Avenue and were out of view for a moment. She had been dying all evening to kiss him, and kiss him properly. For now the brief touch of her lips would have to do. "I especially enjoyed the saxophone player. He was sensational."

Dean seemed to stare at her mouth before sighing and continuing on with their walk home. "He wasn't the only one that was sensational there tonight." His heated glance raked her body. "I had seen that dress on the mannequin in Laura's Boutique window, and I thought it was pretty. But pretty doesn't begin to describe what you look like in it." He shook his head and glanced at her legs. "Talk about sensational."

She grinned, leaned closer, and whispered seductively, "Try saying that to me once we ditch our chaperons."

"Yeah?" he countered in a playful whisper. "What are you going to do if I do?"

She gave him a look that should have melted his kneecaps and left him in absolutely no doubt

Silver in the Moonlight
151

where she wanted this evening to end—in his bed. She was tired of waiting and she really didn't care if Ida would consider her "brazen." "You'd be surprised what I'd do."

After delivering that promising statement, she called up to her aunts. "So, you two, what did you think of the saxophone player?" She ignored Dean's low groan, which had nothing to do with her calling to her aunts and everything to do with her intentions.

Sadie and Ida both slowed their steps and waited for her and Dean to catch up. "We enjoyed him and the rest of the band very much," Sadie said, "but we can't wait until next Saturday night. It's going to be big-band music."

"Did you hear that, Dean? Big-band music."

"I heard." Dean's voice had a rough edge to it, as if he were in pain. His arm tightened around the blankets he was carrying, and the gleam in his brown eyes was both hot and hungry. She had a feeling she was going to be getting her wish that night.

Katherine felt herself flush and prayed her aunts didn't notice her heightened color under the glare of the streetlights.

"It's still early, Kitty," Sadie said as they stopped at the edge of crushed-shell driveway that led to their house. "Why don't you and Dean go take a walk or a nice drive?"

Ida looked ready to protest such an outrageous suggestion, but Sadie, not so subtly, nudged her sister with her elbow.

Dean handed Sadie her blanket. "That's an excellent idea. I don't know why I hadn't thought of it myself."

"Good." Sadie's smile couldn't have been wider if she had just won a blue ribbon in a pie-baking contest. "We'll leave the kitchen door unlocked for you, Kitty." She grabbed hold of Ida's elbow and started to pull her older sister toward the house. "Good night, Dean."

Ida glared at Sadie, but did manage a thin smile for Katherine and Dean. "Good night, you two."

"Good night," Katherine called, trying desperately not to smile at Sadie's obvious matchmaking and Ida's obvious disapproval.

"Good night, Sadie and Ida." Dean took her hand and pulled her along the sidewalk toward his house. He stopped just past the rose-covered fence and watched from the shadows as both of her aunts made it safely into their home and closed the door behind them.

She couldn't help but be touched by his concern for her aunts. Dean Katz had to be the sweetest thing since Sadie's peach pie. If she hadn't already discovered she was in love with the man, that simple caring gesture would have lit the bulb in her brain.

"So what will it be?" he asked. "A walk or a drive?"

"Neither."

"Neither?" She could feel his gaze search her face. "You have something else in mind?"

Oh, she definitely had something else in mind. The problem was she couldn't come right out and say it. It just didn't seem appropriate to say things like deep kisses, hot skin, and cool sheets to Dean. Instead she nodded toward his house. "How about some coffee?"

"Coffee? What is with you and coffee?" He laughed good-naturedly. "If I didn't know better, I'd swear you only come over for the caffeine fix." He took her hand again and led her toward his porch.

She liked the feel of his fingers entwined with hers. They were warm and strong. She had to wonder what they would feel like roaming her body. "I usually don't drink this much coffee back home. I guess it's psychological. Just knowing I can't have a cup of "real" coffee at my aunts' makes me crave it all the more."

He opened the front door and ushered her in. "Do you really want me to put on a pot?" Light flared in the hall as he flipped the switch.

"No." She truly wasn't in the mood for coffee. She wanted something a little more stimulating. She wanted Dean.

"Would you like to sit on the upstairs' porch and watch the river?"

That still wasn't it, but it was a move in the right direction—upstairs. She had been in Jasper for over two weeks and so far hadn't managed to see the second floor of Dean's house. "That sounds lovely." She placed her hat on the newel post and preceded Dean up the oak stairs.

The porch ran the entire length of the back of his house and was screened from floor to ceiling. Rattan furniture with brightly colored cushions was arranged so that every seat offered a striking view of the river. Two wall fixtures gave enough light to see where you were walking, but weren't so bright that they distracted from the view. Huge potted palms filled in the areas where there wasn't any furniture. Three white and brass ceiling fans would offer a breeze on hot airless days. She could see miles of the Combahee River rolling its way around the bend, heading for St. Helena Sound.

"This is a wonderful room, Dean." She walked the length of it and studied her aunts' house from this vantage point. It appeared depressingly bleak and dark. She made a mental note to talk to her aunts about outdoor lighting. The sixty-watt bulb burning above the kitchen door barely cut through the darkness, let alone the forest of trees that surrounded the house. "Ralph Chesney stopped by this afternoon and delivered his estimate."

Dean walked up behind her and gazed at her aunts' house. "How did they take the news?"

"Amazingly well." She still couldn't fathom it. "I expected Sadie and Ida to have near heart fail-

Silver in the Moonlight

ure at the final price, but they both gave the impression that they weren't too concerned."

"Your aunts happen to be my bank's wealthiest clients, Kate. I don't think the financial end was one of their concerns."

"In a way it was." She didn't want to tell Dean about their plans for her future. For some strange reason, it made her feel selfish. "I think they've been talking to some of their friends who had extensive work done. They knew beforehand what kind of money the repairs would cost, so they were well prepared for the shock of seeing the estimate."

"Are they going to get the work done?"

She shrugged. "I think so, but they're not saying right now. They told me they want to discuss it privately before committing to anything." She tried to visualize what the house would look like when it was done, and couldn't. The overgrown trees and surrounding gardens would still be blocking the view. "I wonder if Ida would allow me to call in a landscaper to give them an estimate on thinning out the jungle and making the gardens a little more manageable."

"An estimate wouldn't harm anything, but first you would have to find a landscaper that Ida would approve of." Dean turned her away from the screen and motioned for her to sit on one of the couches. "No more talk about your aunts tonight." He sat down on the opposite end of the couch. "I really like Sadie and Ida, Kate, don't get me wrong. It's just that I would love to know more about you. What's your favorite color? What kind of music do you listen to?" He shrugged, smiling. "What do you want out of life?"

She almost laughed. What did she want out of life? That was like asking someone the meaning of life. How did a person know what she wanted out of life, until she'd actually lived it. Usually by then it was too late. She knew what she wanted right this minute, but for the rest of her life? That was the tricky part. "I guess I want what everybody else wants."

"What's that?"

"To be happy." She kicked off her sandals and tucked her feet up under the flowing skirt of the sundress. She wondered if Dean was thinking that eventually she would have to go home. Home to Boston. Boston, where the winters were cold and lonely. Boston, where her family was, at least part of her family. The other part, a pair of sweet aunts, was safely tucked away below the Mason-Dixon Line. Winters in Jasper held a lot more promise. So did the vacant store down on Main Street. "I don't want to be eighty years old and sitting on some nursing-home porch muttering about things in my life I should have done and didn't. I don't want to live with regrets."

Dean turned and faced her. "Name something you would possibly regret later in life."

It was a teasing question, one meant to dis-

Silver in the Moonlight

cover something about her. She could think of a couple different responses to it, all of them safe and ordinary. *I want to see the aurora borealis. I want to visit Kathmandu. I want to swim naked in the Pacific Ocean. I want a family of my own.* She was tired of being safe and ordinary. She wanted something more. Needed something more.

She glanced down at her hands in her lap and noticed they were trembling slightly. Her father had once claimed she had nerves of steel. Maybe they weren't made of steel, just silver like her name. Silver could be bent under the right pressure. She looked up at Dean and told him what had been keeping her up at night since her second day in Jasper. "I would regret never making love with you."

Dean didn't blink. In fact he didn't even seem to breathe. He just sat there staring at her with eyes darkened to near black with desire. She could see the white-knuckled grip he had on the back of the sofa. When he finally moved, she expected him to haul her into his arms and kiss her. Instead he practically jumped off the couch and sprinted to the other side of the porch.

Ten feet of space separated them when he finally spoke. "There's a lot about me you don't know, Kate."

"I know everything I need to know." He was right. There probably was a whole bunch of stuff she didn't know about him. Stuff she couldn't have cared less about right now. She knew she had fallen in love with him. She knew he held a good job, had a gorgeous home, and liked his coffee strong and black. She also knew he possessed a heart of gold. His loving concern for her aunts and this town proved that point over and over. He was also a gentleman.

"Do you know why I moved to Jasper and bought the bank?"

She frowned as the possibilities whirled through her mind. "I would assume you were interested in purchasing a bank and Jasper's was available."

"No." He stared at her as he thrust his hand through his hair. "I mean yes. I was interested in owning my own bank and yes, Jasper's was available." He seemed distracted that she had answered his question correctly. "But why was I interested in owning a bank?"

"Banking's in your blood. Your father's a banker and so was your grandfather. Aren't you the one who told me it's tradition in the South to follow in your father's footsteps? Wasn't that the reason why my father and grandfather had a parting of the ways?" She couldn't understand what all of this had to do with making love. All she wanted was Dean's hot kisses and for him not to stop that night. Was that too much to ask for?

"Yes, banking's in my blood, Kate. But I already was a vice-president in my father's banks. I was handling numerous responsibilities and other people's money and I was earning a lot more than I do now."

"So why did you give it all up?"

"Who said I gave it all up?" He turned away and stared out into the night. "My father fired me."

"For what?" Dear Lord, what had Dean done that his own father fired him? There was only one thing she could think of that would cause that action—embezzlement. People with hearts of gold didn't embezzle from banks. Dean couldn't be owning his own bank if he had embezzled from someone else's. Dean wasn't a criminal.

"I was involved in a nasty scandal."

She frowned at the way his shoulders slumped. She wanted to walk over to him and press her cheek against his back. Dean looked like he could use a friend. "It must have been a humdinger if your father fired you from the bank."

"Oh, it was." He glanced over his shoulder at her. "You're going to want to hear about it, aren't you?"

A sick knot of dread twisted in her gut. For some reason, this scandal was connected with her blatant proposition to make love. She was curious as to what it might be, but it didn't change her feelings or her desire. She still wanted to make love with Dean. "If you want to tell me, I'll listen. But it won't change what I feel, Dean."

His gaze burned into hers, seeking her soul.

She sat there and met his eyes, and gave him her soul.

"It's not a pretty story."

"I imagine it's not."

He was silent for a long time, then he began. "The one thing I did well back in Charleston was work. I worked fourteen-hour days, seven days a week. I took up golf just so I could work the greens and the clubhouses. I started at the bottom in my father's banks. I rose to the position of vice-president, not because I was Jonathan Katz's son, but because of the work I had done. I'm very proud of that fact. The social circles in Charleston meant nothing to me except to offer me another opportunity to work. I was basically what you would refer to as a nerd. All work and no play definitely made Dean a very dull boy."

She couldn't imagine Dean being a dull boy if her life depended on it. He was the most exciting man she had ever met, and he was taking this story a mite too seriously. He needed to lighten up. "You don't kiss like a dull boy."

Dean seemed to stumble over his next thought. He finally looked at her, gave a small smile, and said, "Thanks."

She returned his smile with a full-blown grin. "You're welcome."

He glanced away from her again. "One evening my parents hosted a party. As was common, it was partly social, partly business. Everyone who was anyone in Charleston was there. By midnight

Silver in the Moonlight

I had closed a deal I had been working on for nearly a month. I wanted to celebrate, so I retired to my father's den and helped myself to some of his private stock of Scotch. I was on my second glass when Lorna Prescot walked in and tried her hand at seduction."

"Seduction?" The word left an awful taste in her mouth.

"Yeah, seduction." He gazed out toward the river. "The next thing I knew, I was on my third Scotch, Lorna was on my lap with her dress hiked up to her waist, and we were playing tonsil hockey."

"Sounds to me you were playing more than just tonsil hockey." She didn't want to think about Dean with some half-dressed woman sitting on his lap and her tongue halfway down his throat.

"It was only a kiss, but all the signals were there and they were all flashing green. Three drinks, a cause for celebration, and the most willing female straddling my lap. There would have been only one natural conclusion to the evening." He speared his fingers through his hair. "Next thing I knew the door opened and my father and Lorna's father walked into the den, and all hell broke loose."

She arched an eyebrow. "I can imagine." Why had this Lorna person almost gotten the natural conclusion when all she got was frustration? Ten minutes earlier she had been so frustrated that she'd actually asked Dean to make love with her, and what did she receive? A story featuring the lovely Lorna trying to pull a hat trick on his tonsils.

"Lorna started to cry. Her father demanded to know what was going on, as if it hadn't be apparent. My father looked angry and hurt. I went from being embarrassed to shocked when Lorna told her father that our affair had been going on for quite a while. As I stood there paralyzed she informed us all that she was pregnant. My father told Lorna not to worry, that I would do the honorable thing and marry her. A Katz always took responsibility for his action.

"I wiped the growing smile off Lorna's face when I told her, my father, and her father that there hadn't been any affair and that I would not marry her. Lorna did a masterful job of pretending to faint. Her father took a swing at me, which luckily I blocked, and my father, totally at a loss as to what to do with me since I'd never been in trouble a day in my life, tried to send me to my room."

She laughed out loud. She couldn't help herself. The scene he had painted was just too vivid. Dean's father had tried to send his grown son, a vice-president at his banks, to his room.

Dean glared at her. "It wasn't that funny!"

She pressed her hand against her stomach, hoping to hold the next outburst of laughter in. "How old were you?"

Silver in the Moonlight

"Thirty-two." He turned his back on her once again, but not before she saw a tiny smile curving his mouth. "The Prescots were my father's wealthiest clients. I told her father that the baby wasn't mine. Couldn't be mine. That I had never been intimate with his daughter and that the kiss they had just interrupted had been the first time I had ever touched her."

"How did they take that?"

"How do you think? Lorna had regained consciousness and was lying on the sofa like some Victorian virgin swooning at my every word. Her father demanded that I do the honorable thing and give his grandchild my name. I refused and my father fired me on the spot."

"Your father believed Lorna over you?" She couldn't imagine what that must have done to Dean.

"He chose to believe the daughter of his wealthiest client over his own son, yes." Dean turned back around and studied her face. "The entire town was scandalized and to this day my name is the equivalent of mud in most social circles."

"Why? The baby wasn't yours. She lied."

"Are you sure about that?"

"Of course I'm sure. You would have married her immediately, before anyone else learned about the pregnancy." She knew Dean well enough to realize that. He never would have left a woman alone who was carrying his child. He *would* have done the honorable thing.

He smiled. "Thank you for the vote of confidence. It was more than my father gave me." He shrugged and told her the rest of the story. "I left Charleston, bought the Jasper bank, and moved here. Immediately after Lorna's baby was born blood tests proved I couldn't have been the father. My father sent a fax informing me that my position of vice-president had been reinstated effective immediately and that I was to take over the Beaufort branch office."

She knew how the story ended. "You refused the offer and have been here ever since."

"In a nutshell, yes."

She now understood why Jasper had become so important to Dean. If the town prospered, so would the bank. He needed to prove to his father that he could make it on his own. Dean's actions weren't so different from her own.

She also understood why he felt the need to tell her about the scandal in his past. If Lorna had shouted from the rooftops that Dean was the father of her baby and that he refused to marry her, society would have crucified him and no blood test after the fact would have cleaned the slate. If Katherine understood one thing, she understood the workings of high society. In many people's minds, Dean would always be guilty of not honoring his responsibilities. She couldn't think of a worse insult to hurl at him.

Silver in the Moonlight

She slowly stood up and walked across the porch to join him. "Did you really think that story was going to change the way I feel?"

"I wanted you to hear it before we took the next step."

She read the hope and need burning deep in his eyes and relaxed. He wasn't going to stop tonight. There weren't going to be any more barriers between them. She stepped closer. The scent of his aftershave tantalized her senses. The heat radiating from his body pulled her nearer. She raised her hand and outlined the shape of his lips with her finger. "What is our next step?" She wanted to hear the words his eyes were promising.

He captured her hand and placed tiny kisses on the tip of each finger before scraping his teeth over the pounding pulse in her wrist. "Ravishment."

She closed her eyes as his mouth worked its way up her arm and he nuzzled the sensitive spot on the inside of her elbow. "Whose? Yours or mine?" Desire thundered through her veins like a locomotive out of control. She could feel her knees grow weak as she reached for him.

He released her arm and hauled her against his chest. "Both." His mouth skimmed her jaw. "Tell me again that this is what you want, Kate."

She wrapped her arms around his neck and stood on her toes. Her lips brushed his. "I would much rather show you, Dean."

Dean's hungry growl echoed across the porch and he swung her up into his arms. As he carried her back into the house she locked her arms around his neck and teased the pulse point at the base of his throat with her tongue. He tasted like sweet night air and fire.

A minute later she was in his bedroom being lowered to her feet. The hallway light spilled into the room, casting everything in shadows. She gave the room a quick glance and came away with the impression it suited Dean. Light-colored walls, sheer curtains at the windows, and dark heavy furniture. Her gaze landed on the wide and high four-poster bed. A person would need a running start to leap up on top of the mattress, or the use of the footstool placed beside the bed. She smiled at Dean. "Do you have insurance in case I fall off?"

He brushed her hair back from her face. "I won't let you fall off." His fingers trailed down the side of her neck. "I'll be holding on to you real tight."

"Promise?" She took a step closer to him. Fire flared everywhere his fingers touched.

His mouth blazed a trail up her throat and across her jaw. His voice was a roughened growl as he nipped at her lower lip and forced her to open her mouth. "Promise," he murmured.

Katherine welcomed the heat of his mouth and the bold thrust of his tongue. The wait was over. Her hands eagerly pulled his shirt from the waistband of his pants. She felt Dean's fingers slide the zipper of her dress down as she broke the kiss and pulled his shirt up and over his head.

His mouth crushed hers as he pushed the dress off her shoulders and it pooled at her feet. Her fingers trembled as she undid his belt and reached for the clasp on his pants. His hands captured hers, pulling them away from the front of his pants and placing them on his chest. Dark golden curls tickled her fingers as she ran them back down over his stomach.

He sucked in a ragged breath. "We have to slow down, Kate."

She pressed her lips against his thundering heart as the back fastening of her bra came undone. She shrugged her shoulders and the white lace garment landed on top of her dress. She was standing in the circle of Dean's arms wearing nothing but a pair of panties and a spritz of perfume she had purchased in town the other morning, called Southern Seduction. Her lips found a dark nipple buried beneath a cover of curls and gave it a gentle tug. "Name one good reason." She didn't want to take it slow and easy. She had waited too long. Her mouth went in search of the other nipple.

Dean groaned and cupped her bottom. His fingers slipped into the waistband of her panties and started to slide them down over her hips. "I want to remember the first time we make love."

She skimmed her mouth down his chest as she

fumbled with the brass tab of his zipper. "You'll remember it, Dean. I promise."

In a burst of motion, he swept her panties down her legs and swung her up into his arms. "What are you doing to me, you little witch?" He took three steps to the bed, pulled down the covers, and lightly tossed her onto the middle of the mattress.

She bounced slightly and grinned as Dean kicked off his shoes and started to remove his own pants. "Gee, Dean, what happened to your Southern charm? Calling me a witch wasn't very gentlemanly, especially since I live so close to Salem."

He halted in the middle of pulling off his socks to stare at her. He must have noticed her grin because he shook his head and muttered, "Definitely a witch," before removing the other sock and joining her on the bed.

The explosion of desire was instantaneous. His mouth pulled a wild cry from her as he cupped one of her breasts and raked his thumb across the nipple. Her hands stroked his back and raced over his lean hips. His arousal nudged her thigh and she instinctively pressed her hips against him. Desire sped through her body like wildfire. She had never felt anything so primitive, so promising.

The sensation of emptiness building between her thighs was excruciating. She wanted Dean to fill the void. Only he could arouse such emotions,

Silver in the Moonlight

such heat. Only he could fulfill the promise his body was making. "Now, Dean," she begged as she arched her back once more. "I need you now." She reached for his shaft and tried to complete their union.

Dean rolled away, reaching across the bed toward something in a drawer of the nightstand. She heard him open the drawer and fumble around the sound of ripping foil. In a moment he was once again reaching for her. Strong fingers burrowed through the curls at the juncture of her thighs and sought the liquid fire burning there.

Her hips pressed against his hand as she cupped his muscular buttocks and urged him closer. She was near to climaxing, but she wanted him deep inside when she went over the edge. She wanted Dean with her, all the way. She wrapped her legs around his hips and nipped at his lower lip.

His groan came from deep in his chest as he removed his hand and in one quick thrust filled her. Her legs tightened their grip as she pulled his mouth down to hers.

She felt him start to pull out and cried, "No, don't." She would die if he left her now.

His mouth left frantic little kisses on every available inch of her face. "I'm not leaving you, Kate." He arched his back and filled her once again. "I couldn't leave you now if the bed caught on fire."

She met his next thrust with one of her own.

The heat built higher and the pace quickened. "Hurry, Dean. . . ." She gasped for breath as the thrusting rhythm turned wild. "I want you with me."

He gripped her hips and drove deeper. "I'm with you, Kate."

She cried out his name as she felt the ground disappear beneath her and she was whirled over the edge. She vaguely heard Dean call her name over and over as blinding swirls of darkness stole her breath and released her from the passion.

Two hours later Dean backed Kate up against her aunts' kitchen door and kissed her until he felt her melt against him. Lord, what had she done to him? Katherine Silver was indeed a witch. He was about to take her again right there on Sadie and Ida's porch. The two times they had made love in his bed hadn't been enough. He was getting the strangest feeling that he would never get enough of Kate.

He broke the kiss and tenderly cupped her flushed cheek. "I want you back in my bed."

She placed a kiss in the center of his palm. "I want that, too, but you know I can't stay." She nodded toward the house behind her. "Sadie and Ida wouldn't understand."

"Just because I know that doesn't mean I have to like it." He understood Kate's concern. Sadie and Ida were from a different era. They would

Silver in the Moonlight

never condone their niece sleeping at his house. It was just one of the many problems facing this relationship. The other more pressing problem was Kate living in Boston and his knowing that eventually she would have to head home.

He leaned down and kissed her again. When a moan of desire purred in her throat, he released her. "Will I see you in the morning?" Why was it so hard to let her go in?

"Sadie and Ida leave for church around eight-thirty." She turned the knob and opened the door.

She looked about as reluctant to leave him as he felt about leaving her. If he couldn't say good night for one night, a mere six and a half hours, how was he going to handle it when she went back to Boston?

He brushed a quick kiss over her still swollen lips. He grew harder just thinking about the things she had done with that delectable mouth of hers. He gently pushed her into the house before he did something incredibly stupid, like dragging her back across the yards and tying her to his bedpost for the next twenty years or so. "Good night, sweet Kate. I'll have the coffee waiting."

He didn't step off the porch until she had whispered her good night and closed and locked the door behind her. With a weary sigh he headed back across the yard and to his bed. His very big and empty bed.

NINE

Katherine glanced away from Dean and tried not to remember how they had spent the entire morning in his bed and that half of everything they'd done was probably illegal in one state or another. Dean possessed the most talented hands, and his mouth . . . Lord, his mouth should be registered as a deadly weapon with the intent to kill with pleasure. What that man had done with his mouth was—

"Kitty, are you all right?" Sadie asked.

Katherine looked at her aunt and blinked. She could feel the heat of the memories sweeping up her face and avoided Dean's gaze. "What did you say?" She had absolutely no idea what her aunt had asked.

"I asked if you were all right." Sadie leaned across the table and tried to get a better look at

Silver in the Moonlight

her. "You seem mighty flushed. It's not too hot in here, is it?"

"No, Sadie, I'm fine, the temperature is fine." She resisted the urge to fan herself with her napkin. Her aunts really should check into getting central air installed during the renovations. For some reason, it had turned awfully warm in the kitchen. She glanced at the table, laden with the remains of Sunday dinner, and offered her aunt a small smile. "Everything was delicious, as always."

Dean had wanted to take her out for dinner, but Sadie and Ida had insisted that they both eat dinner with them. They said they had something very important to discuss. So far the conversation had revolved around ordinary things—the weather, the ridiculous hat Eleanor Crabtree had worn to church that morning, and the latest missing flowers from Ida's gardens. She could tell Dean was having a hard time believing anyone would steal Ida's flowers, but earlier she, too, had noticed the missing flowers. Something definitely was going on in Ida's gardens at night.

Ida stood up and started to clear the table. Dean gallantly took the plates out of Ida's hands and carried them to the sink. "Kate and I will do the dishes. You two prepared the meal, we'll clean up."

Katherine reached for the platter holding the rest of the Sunday ham. "You two go sit out back and enjoy the view. When Dean and I are done in here, we'll join you and then you can discuss whatever it is you two wanted to talk to us about." She ignored her aunts' protests and shooed them both out the back door.

Minutes later she was filling the sink with hot soapy water while Dean alternated between bringing over dishes and nibbling on the back of her neck. She guiltily glanced toward the screen door every time he came within touching distance. Sadie might understand about physical attraction. By the merry twinkle that was in her aunt's eyes every time Dean and Katherine were together, not only did Sadie understand, she apparently approved wholeheartedly. Ida was a different story. Ida had a very old-fashioned, yet dear, way of looking at things. Katherine had to respect her aunts' feelings on the subject of male-female relationships.

With growing frustration, and threatening Dean with retaliation, they finished cleaning up the kitchen and joined her aunts at the table and chairs under the ancient oak near the river's edge.

Katherine didn't like the way her aunts fidgeted and glanced at each other when they thought they weren't being watched. Something was up, something big.

She took a seat and gave her aunts a reassuring smile. "The kitchen is once again in order." Dean took the empty seat next to her. His knee bumped hers and she jerked her leg out of his way. Ida looked anxious enough without learning

Silver in the Moonlight

that her niece was playing footsie with their next-door neighbor. "What did you two want to talk to us about?" She had thought it was about the renovations, but she couldn't comprehend why her aunts would insist that Dean be present to hear their decision.

Sadie glanced at Ida and received a slight nod to proceed. "We've been thinking quite a lot about all the renovations the house needs. We really would love to see the house brought back to its former glory."

"We don't like having to run up into the attic every time it rains to put buckets under the leaks," added Ida.

Katherine nodded. She knew her aunts had been catching the rainwater from the number of plastic buckets scattered throughout the attic's rooms.

"We also know that the house is way too big for the two of us." Sadie reached for Ida's hand. "Ida shouldn't be climbing all of those stairs. Last month, when she was at the doctor's, he recommended that she move her bedroom to the first floor."

"Why haven't you?" Katherine was stunned to learn that her aunts weren't following the doctor's orders. "Surely you could have found or hired someone to move down the bedroom furniture. With a little help you could have turned the back parlor, which you hardly ever use, into a bedroom."

"Why didn't you ask me to help?" Dean said. "You both know I would have moved down the furniture." He frowned at Ida. "When you came home from that doctor's visit I remember asking you if everything was all right. You told me everything was just fine."

"I didn't lie," said Ida. "The doctor did tell me everything was fine. He was just concerned with the number of times I have to climb the stairs every day." Ida glanced at Sadie. "It's not the bedroom so much. It's the bathroom. We don't have one on the first floor."

Why hadn't she thought of that before? Katherine asked herself. Her aunts' house had only one bathroom and it was on the second floor. The way her aunts were talking it was beginning to sound like they might be considering moving into a smaller, more manageable house. She couldn't imagine her aunts not living here. A Silver had been living in that house since before the Civil War. It would be a sin to break the tradition now just because it didn't have a downstairs bathroom. "I can call Ralph Chesney first thing in the morning and see what it would cost to add a bathroom downstairs and to convert the back parlor into a bedroom for Ida."

Sadie and Ida exchanged a smile. "We want to call Mr. Chesney about some other things too."

"Like what?" Katherine sighed with relief and the tension in her shoulders dissipated. Her aunts were still interested in living here.

Silver in the Moonlight

"We decided," declared Sadie, "that we would really like to open up our home as a bed-and-breakfast."

Two and a half hours later Dean stood with Kate at Jasper's docks. After having a lengthy discussion with Sadie and Ida, they had gone for a walk and had ended up on the far side of town. Fishing was still the main livelihood of many of Jasper's residents. In the past year charter fishing boats had nearly surpassed the number used for the fishing industry. Two new piers had been added and two empty and abandoned warehouses were now being used to hold various businesses, from bait shops, to an outboard-motor repair shop, to a sporting-goods store. Captain John's Diner had opened the previous fall and was a huge success. Plans were already in the works for another seafood restaurant to open by midsummer. Jasper was indeed booming.

The shrieking cry of a circling seagull pulled his attention from the bobbing boats and up into the night sky. He liked the daytime hours, from his early-morning jog, to putting in a full day's work, to relaxing on his porch. But he loved the nights the most. There was something about the peaceful nights in Jasper that connected with his soul. He reached for Kate's hand and nibbled on the tips of her fingers. It was the same connection that Kate made. She had touched his soul and he would rather give up the tranquil nights in Jasper than give up Kate.

He knew she had to go back to Boston eventually and he had been giving a lot of thought to what it might cost to buy into the banking business up there. His gut was telling him it would probably be a lot more expensive than this little Jasper bank owner could afford. He ran the tip of his tongue over her palm and to the rapidly beating pulse point at her wrist. Oh well, with his credentials he could always apply for a position in someone else's bank.

She pulled her hand out of his grasp and glanced around. "Stop that," she hissed. "Someone might see us."

"Let them." He wrapped his arm around her shoulders, not caring who might see them together, and started walking back toward the center of town. If they hurried they could make it to Sandy's Ice Cream Parlor before it closed at ten. He suddenly had a craving for cold ice cream and Kate's hot kisses.

"So you think your aunts' idea of opening their own bed-and-breakfast is a good one?" He had seen Kate's enthusiasm grow as her aunts laid out their plans. He had to admit, with Kate's suggestions, the idea wasn't quite as astonishing as it had been when they had first suggested it.

"I think it would do them a world of good. Sadie would have someone to bake for and Ida can work in the gardens and supply fresh flowers." Kate leaned closer to him as they turned back down Main Street.

"I think you're right about having Chesney draw up some plans to have both of your aunts' bedrooms moved downstairs, add a full bath, and turn the glass sunroom into their private living space. The front parlor and dining room will be for the guests and the rest of the downstairs would be off-limits."

Kate was once again drawn into the plans. "On the second floor the master bedroom and the small bedroom next to it could be converted into a nice-size suite, and then there are the other two bedrooms." She wrapped her arm around his waist and hugged him as her enthusiasm grew.

"The bath that's up there," he added, "now needs to be completely redone, so it would be a simple process to split it and make two separate baths for those rooms. That way all the rooms will have their own baths. It's a major plus in the bed-and-breakfast business." He had seen quite a few of the older homes turned into bed-and-breakfasts over the past eighteen months, and was pretty confident about the finer selling points. As far as he could see, Sadie and Ida's large home had great potential.

"What do you think of the attic?" Kate asked. "I was thinking they could get two bedrooms, each with a small, yet quaint bathroom. With those dormers overlooking the river they could be a fantastic pair of rooms. That would bring the number of rooms available to five. Do you think that would be too much?"

"I think Sadie would be in her glory wiping up cinnamon rolls faster than the Pillsbury Dough Boy and Ida would have an endless army of vases to fill. It would be unusual for all five rooms to be taken at the same time, but it could happen during the peak tourist season. Winters down here are kind of slow, but things pick up around the last week in March and then die back down around the end of October."

"You don't think I hurt their feelings when I insisted they hire someone to clean the rooms? I don't want Ida climbing the stairs and Sadie would never get any baking done if she had to scrub toilets and change linens all day long."

Dean pulled her into a recessed doorway and kissed her the way he had been thinking about doing since joining her for dinner at her aunts'. Only Kate would think she might have hurt someone's feelings by insisting they hire a cleaning person. He felt her melt into his embrace and backed her against the wooden doors of Jasper's hardware store.

He groaned in frustration as she obviously remembered where they were and gently pushed him away. His house, and bed, was still a ten-minute walk away and his body felt on fire. Whatever flavor of ice cream he decided on, it surely would be melted before they reached the privacy of his house. He tried to remember if he

Silver in the Moonlight

had any ice cream in the freezer. He didn't think he did. He'd had to give up buying ice cream as soon as he tasted Sadie's chocolate-chip cookies.

Kate stepped out of the shadows and back onto the sidewalk. He chuckled at the way she nervously glanced up and down the street. "Come on, Kate, I'll treat you to an ice-cream cone if you promise to let me finish that kiss once we get back to my place."

Her laugh wrapped its way around his heart as she took his hand and started to walk. "I don't know, Dean." She tried to look thoughtful, but ruined the image by grinning. "It would have to be an awfully impressive ice-cream cone."

He saw another couple walking toward them, so he bent down and whispered, "I'll give you my word, as a gentleman, that you will be duly impressed."

Kate was still blushing wildly as the other couple strolled past.

Twenty minutes later Kate used her tongue to capture the melting ice cream running down the side of her cone. She ignored Dean's playful groans of agony and concentrated on savoring every drop of her butter-pecan ice cream. Dean's bank was right up the street and they were approaching the vacant store with the orange "For Rent" sign still taped to the big window. Her feet naturally stopped in front of the window and she stared in at the darkness.

"Isn't this the same window I saw you looking in the other day?" Dean glanced over her shoulder and into the dark store. "You mentioned something about your future. Are you still seeing it?"

"Yes, I do believe I am." She raised her fingers to the orange sign and lightly tapped on the glass.

"What exactly are you seeing in there?" Dean pressed his nose against the glass and looked harder.

"I see Jasper's first travel agency." She was going to do it. The decision had been made. She was staying in Jasper.

He started to chuckle and shake his head. "A travel agency? How in the world do you see . . ." His voice trailed off as he turned and faced her. "You're going to open up your own travel agency?"

She had to smile at the look of astonishment on his face. Either the idea totally shocked him, or he didn't think she was capable of starting her own business. She'd give him the benefit of the doubt and assume it had never occurred to him that she might open up a travel agency in Jasper. "I've been thinking about it and I really can't come up with any reason why I shouldn't. I was starting to get restless working for the company I've been employed with for five years. It's a real

Silver in the Moonlight

nice company and I love the people, but something has been missing. Your letter concerning my aunts came at a very opportune time. I needed this time away from the job so I could step back and examine what the problem might be."

She nodded toward the shop. "It occurred to me the other day that I really do enjoy the travel industry and I didn't want to leave it. There are more travel agencies in Boston than the city needs. I decided to open mine right here in downtown Jasper. It would solve a lot of problems, like giving me the chance to rediscover my Southern roots and keep an eye on Sadie and Ida."

"You're staying!" Dean glanced up and down the street, muttered a word that sounded suspiciously like a curse, and started to drag her toward Jackson Avenue and his house. He barely nodded in greeting to Reverend Frost and his wife, who were out for an evening stroll. Under his breath he kept muttering, "I can't believe you're staying."

Katherine ditched her ice-cream cone in a trash can and managed a slight waving of her fingers to the reverend and his missus. By the stunned look on Reverend Frost's face, she wouldn't be surprised if Sadie and Ida got a call in the morning. Dean was acting like a Neanderthal man dragging her off to his cave. She should be counting her blessings that he wasn't pulling her down the sidewalk by her hair.

It was awfully sweet of him to be so excited about her staying in Jasper, but she had a funny feeling deep within her gut that he hadn't heard one word about her travel agency. He had only heard she was staying.

As they turned down Jackson Avenue she knew where he was taking her and why. He wanted to celebrate her decision in the privacy of his home, not in the middle of downtown. She was all for his idea of a celebration. In fact she had been about to suggest it when he had taken the matter into his own hands and practically dragged her down the street.

She grinned as he jogged up his front steps and pushed open his front door. The door had barely closed when he hauled her into his arms and kissed her with such pent-up emotions, she had no other alternative but to melt into him.

A moment later cool wooden flooring pressed against her back, and clothing was scattered around the foyer. Somewhere along the way to the floor she'd forgotten how to breathe. She didn't care. Breathing wasn't important. Loving Dean was.

Katherine used Dean's arm as a pillow and allowed the afternoon sun to deepen the tan on her back and legs. The past week had proved to be a very hectic one. Ralph Chesney had been called back and new price quotes were in the

Silver in the Moonlight

works. The empty store on Main Street was now legally hers, at least for the next twelve months. The painters would be starting on Monday and new carpeting had been ordered. All morning, while Dean had worked his bank's Saturday hours, she had helped Ida in the gardens.

Her life in Jasper was filled with contentment and happiness. Everything she had ever wanted out of life was right here in this small Southern town. Her family was here. Her aunts loved her unconditionally, something her own parents couldn't bring themselves to do. Her career was now here and soon she would be seeing to the residents' hopes and dreams of their own perfect vacations. But most important, Dean was here.

The man she loved was lying beside her. Life couldn't be any better. Well, maybe one little thing more and her life would be perfect. Dean still hadn't told her that he loved her. Three little words and that nagging voice in the back of her head would be silenced. She wanted those words.

She opened her eyes and studied Dean's profile. His eyes were closed against the glare of the sun. His skin held the rich tan of Southern living and contrasted perfectly with the washed-out pastel colors of the quilt they were lying on. The shadow dusting his jaw looked sexy as all get-out and she was tempted to tease the stubble with a hundred little kisses.

The thick forest of trees and shrubs on her aunts' property, along with Dean's exquisitely landscaped gardens, gave them plenty of privacy. No one could see them basking in the sun unless they were in an airplane or a boat sailing on the river and had a pair of very strong binoculars.

She missed Dean's touch. She hated having to leave his bed almost immediately after they made love. Sadie and Ida never waited up for her, but she knew they were aware of what time she came in every night. Sadie's knowing smile in the morning caused her to blush, but Ida's disapproving frown caused her to worry. She didn't want to hurt her aunts in any way, but she loved Dean. She wanted to sleep in his arms and wake in the morning pressed against his body.

"What are you staring at?" He rubbed at his jaw. "Did I nick myself this morning?"

She leaned over and brushed a kiss along his jaw. "No, I was just admiring the view." She grinned at the slight flush that darkened his cheeks. It never ceased to amaze her how easily her compliments made him flush. "Explain to me again how you walked around Charleston with a bag over your head without running into light posts or moving cars?" It was a joke between them. She still couldn't fathom how he'd managed to stay single and unattached all this time.

The incident with Lorna Prescot didn't count. She'd been after a husband and a father for her unborn child and Dean's good looks hadn't entered the picture. His easygoing attitude, fat wallet, prestigious family name, and big heart did.

Lorna probably thought she had found easy prey with Dean. She had never counted on Dean standing up for the truth and defying his family by not marrying her. Lorna Prescot was a fool.

She playfully skimmed his chest with the tips of her fingers. "The bag wouldn't have fooled me, Dean." His cotton T-shirt was warm beneath her fingers. As her hand angled its way lower Dean groaned, then she was flat on her back with Dean looming over her. It was the position she had been hoping for.

"You're playing with fire, Kate."

She could tell by the desire darkening his eyes that it wouldn't take much more to push him over the edge. She loved it when he slipped over the edge, especially since he always managed to bring her with him. She reached up and cupped his shadowy jaw. "Are you planning on burning me, Dean?"

His fingers traced her jaw, the side of her neck, and outlined the deep V of her halter top. "I'm planning on loving you until we both go up in smoke."

How could she not love this man? She wrapped her arms around his neck and pulled his mouth closer. "Then it's a good thing the river is so close."

His mouth captured hers in a kiss guaranteed to set off fire alarms. Fire indeed rushed through her blood, sending it boiling with need. She met the thrust of his tongue with a riposte of her own.

Heat was building to a dangerous level. Her hands clung to his back, urging him closer.

"Oh my!" Ida exclaimed.

Dean jerked back so fast, he nearly dislocated her arm. "Ida?"

Katherine sat up and stared at her aunt standing in a small clearing not ten feet from them. A vase overflowing with daisies was clutched in her trembling hand. By her pallor, Katherine could tell she was truly upset at finding her niece in such a compromising position. Not that Katherine considered it particularly compromising.

Dean was fully clothed in shorts and a T-shirt. She was still in the same outfit, shorts and a halter top, she had worn all morning when she helped her aunt in the gardens. Yes, they had been sharing a kiss, and on a scale of one to ten, it had been a ten. But still it was only a kiss.

Katherine couldn't bring herself to look at Dean. He had once again been caught playing tonsil hockey with a relative of his bank's wealthiest client, a niece this time instead of a daughter. To Dean it probably was all the same. Except this time she was going to make sure there was a different outcome.

She stood up and brushed an imaginary wrinkle from her shorts. "Are those flowers for Dean, Ida? They look lovely. Did you cut them from the garden out front?" She knew where the flowers had come from. Only one of Ida's gardens had daisies blooming, but she wanted to start a con-

Silver in the Moonlight

versation on any topic that didn't center on kissing and compromising positions.

Ida reluctantly handed her the vase, but continued to glare at Dean. "They were for him. Now I'm not too sure."

Katherine was extremely thankful Ida didn't possess a shotgun. Her aunt probably would have already gone home to get it. "Aunt Ida, Dean wasn't doing anything I didn't want him to do." It sounded so inane, but she didn't know what else to say to her aunt. "I'm sure Dean appreciates the flowers. He has a lovely cherry table in the hallway that these will look wonderful on." She glanced at Dean, who had stood, and offered him a small, hesitant smile and the vase. "Don't you, Dean?"

He took the vase and gave her a funny look before turning to Ida. "You don't have to worry, Ida. I am planning on asking your niece if she would do me the honor of consenting to be my wife."

"You are?" Ida's glare softened into a flush of happiness.

Katherine just stood there in shock as her heart nearly leaped out of her chest. Dean had been planning on asking her to marry him! She grinned at him. True happiness was within her grasp. Everything she had ever wanted in life was standing beside her. So why didn't it feel right?

Her smile faded as her brain finally kicked in, overriding her pounding heart. She knew what the problem was. Dean had never once told her that he loved her. He was writing his own ending to this "minor" scandal. An ending she didn't approve of. She didn't want to trap Dean into marrying her.

He gave her a tender look that nearly convinced her he was telling the truth. "I was planning on doing my proposing in a more private setting, but I guess the setting doesn't matter as much as your answer does."

She felt tears pooling in her eyes and rapidly blinked them away. "Just because Sadie and Ida are your bank's customers doesn't mean you have to do this, Dean." She wanted him to love her for herself, not because of her aunts. Why didn't he tell her that he loved her? She needed the words more than her next breath.

"What do Sadie and Ida have to do with my proposal?" Dean looked thoroughly confused.

"I think they have everything to do with your proposal." She couldn't blink fast enough. Tears overflowed and ran down her cheeks. Dean still hadn't told her that he loved her. If he loved her, surely he would have said the words during a marriage proposal. She had her answer. Dean didn't love her. "As much as I love you, Dean, I can't marry you like this." She turned and fled back toward her aunts' house.

Behind her she heard Dean mutter a word that should have caused Ida to swoon at his feet. Poor Ida had just stood there throughout the

Silver in the Moonlight

whole unpleasant exchange muttering a string of "oh my's." Somewhere on her flight through Ida's overgrown garden Katherine stubbed her toe, but barely noticed. How could she feel a smashed toe when her heart was breaking?

TEN

Dean had paced his front porch and had glared at the joggling board each time he passed it. He had paced every room in the house, but everywhere he went he was reminded of Kate and what he was about to lose. How could he had been so insensitive, so stupid, so blind? He now understood what had upset her so much and why she had fled. At the time all he had heard was her refusal. It had taken a full two minutes and the distant slamming of the screen door before he even realized that she had told him that she loved him. *As much as I love you, Dean, I can't marry you like this.* Kate loved him, and he loved her!

Now, thanks to his speaking before thinking, the woman he loved thought he wanted to marry her to save himself from yet another scandal. Kissing Kate wasn't a scandal. Kissing Kate was his destiny. For the past week he had been thinking about her plans to stay in Jasper and how it would affect them. They couldn't keep sneaking in and out of bed and the thought of never making love with her again was too unbearable even to contemplate. He had figured out four days ago that the only logical thing to do was to get married. He loved her, and he had been pretty sure she loved him. She couldn't possibly react to his every touch the way she did without loving him back.

When Ida had stumbled across them he hadn't given a thought to any ensuing scandal. No one in Jasper, besides Kate's aunts, would care if he had been kissing her. He knew Ida had been upset, which had upset Kate. So instead of defusing the situation, as Kate had been trying to do with her talk about the flowers, he had opened his mouth and assured Ida not to worry, that he was going to be making an honest woman out of her niece. Kate must have been bowled over with his "sensitivity" and his declaration of love. No wonder she had fled in tears.

He must have hurt her terribly. Dean thrust his hand through his hair and left his bedroom. The room held too many memories. His feet carried him to the second-floor screened-in porch. He didn't bother to turn on any lights. What did he need to see? Kate was next door being guarded by a pair of bulldog aunts. Sweet, kind, and gentle Sadie had turned into one stubborn woman when he went over earlier to try to talk to Kate. Sadie had done everything but threaten him with a rolling pin. Ida had stood there pale and teary-eyed, wringing her hands and muttering, "Oh my, oh my." He never even got a glimpse of Kate.

He walked over to the side facing the Silver house and stared out through the screen. It was nearly midnight and all the lights were off. The house appeared to be sleeping. He wondered if Kate was missing him as much as he was missing her. He touched the screen and whispered, "Good night, Kate. Sleep tight." She was so close, yet so far away.

Eventually he would either wear down her guard dogs or catch her outside the house. Sooner or later Kate was going to listen to him, and hopefully he wouldn't end up with his foot in his mouth again. His only fear was that she wouldn't listen to him and would run back to Boston. He'd worry about that later. Right now he knew she was there, sleeping less than fifty yards away from him.

He was just turning from the screen when a faint light in the back garden stopped him. The weak beam of a flashlight was threading its way through Ida's gardens. He could tell by the way the person was moving that he or she didn't want to be seen. Sadie and Ida would never be traipsing through the garden in the dead of night. If it were Kate, she would have no reason to hide her presence.

Whoever was carrying the light was up to no

Silver in the Moonlight

good. There hadn't been any burglaries in Jasper in the entire time he lived there, but that didn't mean it couldn't happen. Sadie and Ida could be hurt . . . and Kate! Cold sweat broke out across his brow and palms as he raced back inside and down the stairs without turning on any lights. Kate would think nothing of confronting a burglar in her aunts' home. His little gutsy love would brandish a fireplace poker and demand that the intruder surrender. If the burglar had thought ahead enough to carry a flashlight, it would stand to reason he also might be carrying a gun.

Dean gave a silent thanks to the oilcan god as he opened his front door without its usual squeak and hurried toward Sadie and Ida's backyard. If he was real lucky he could stop the thief before he reached the house.

Katherine felt the back of her thighs scream in protest from her squatting in the same position for more than twenty minutes. Her hiding spot gave her an excellent view of the entire backyard and most of the side yard. It had been three nights since Ida's flower thief had struck. He, or she, was due, and tonight Katherine was in the mood to put an end to this charade.

Not for a moment did she believe it was a long-dead Confederate soldier. Some flesh-and-blood person was stealing Ida's flowers. Since she knew she wouldn't be able to sleep a wink that night anyway, she decided she would try to stop the flower thief. The only problem was, sitting in the dark by herself gave her too much time to think about Dean and the ugly scene that had happened earlier. Running and hiding in her aunts' house hadn't been such a good idea. It hadn't solved anything, and it hadn't stopped the hurt. She should have listened to her heart and accepted his proposal and the hell with his reasons for asking. Her heart knew only one thing. She loved Dean.

With a silent sigh she went back to concentrating on the matter at hand. She was out to catch a flower thief. She was just about to change her position and risk sitting on the ground when a flash of light on the far side of the garden caught her attention. That solved one mystery. A dead Confederate soldier wouldn't need a light to see by, nor would he even know what a battery-operated flashlight was. Glowing lanterns had been more their style.

She watched as the light made its way around two trees and a tangled mass of tea roses. The insubstantial beam barely outlined what was in its path. There was no way she could distinguish who was holding it. She could see only a dark silhouette that could be a man or a woman. Whoever it was, they were sure taking their good old time making their way through the garden. They seemed to be scouting for the best flowers.

Silver in the Moonlight

Kate stood up and used the lilac bushes to her left as cover as she watched the thief. He stopped in front of the small circular garden that contained a cracked marble birdbath, hundreds of multicolored snapdragons, and spires of blooming canterbury bells. She knew the garden intimately. She had spent a good two hours that morning weeding the thing. Ida loved those flowers. It was going to sadden her immensely in the morning to see that someone had helped himself to her labor of love again.

She watched the thief bend over and start to cut off flowers. It was time to put an end to this. She was going to catch whoever it was redhanded.

She had just taken a step around the lilac bush when she was hauled back against a strong chest and a hand was clamped over her mouth.

"Shhh . . . Kate, it's me, Dean." The hand slowly released her mouth as he continued to whisper in her ear. "What do you think you're doing out here? There's a burglar right over there." He, nodded in the direction of the circular garden.

Katherine reached up and pulled his head lower so she could whisper in his ear. "It's not a burglar. It's Ida's flower thief."

"The Confederate soldier?"

"Nothing so glamourous, just your ordinary run-of-the-mill flower thief." She nodded to her right. "You go that way, and I'll go this way." She pointed to the left. "We'll surround him and put an end to this silliness."

Dean seemed to think about that for a moment before nodding in agreement and slipping off to the right. She headed left.

A minute later Dean stepped out onto the walkway, not four feet from the thief, and growled, "Don't snip another flower!"

Katherine ran forward. Dean should have waited for her instead of confronting the thief on his own. The thief turned and started to hurry away from Dean. "Stop right there!" she shouted.

The thief dropped his flashlight and flowers and raised his hands. "Don't hurt me."

She frowned at the shaky, frightened voice of an old man. Now that she was closer, she could see the thief was indeed an old man.

"Edison? Is that you?" Dean stepped forward and picked up the flashlight.

"I'm sorry, Dean." Edison sounded on the verge of tears.

"Dean, do you know him?"

"Kate, meet Edison Burleigh. He lives about six doors down in the brick Federal-style home. You know, the one with the black iron fence and gate in the front."

"Hello, Edison." She knew the house Dean was referring to. It was one of the other ones Beau Woodrow wanted to turn into a bed-and-breakfast, after sending the owner to a rest home.

Dean had told her Edison wasn't as fortunate as her aunts; he was barely making ends meet with his Social Security checks. "It's nice to finally meet you." She held out her hand. It took a few stunned moments before he accepted her hand.

"Aren't you going to call the police?" Edison's voice trembled on the word *police*.

"No," she said. "I'm sure the police have more important business to handle than a bunch of neighbors getting together in the middle of the night."

Edison studied the walkway for a long time before mumbling, "I was stealing Ida's flowers."

"I'm thinking it was more like borrowing." She couldn't be mad at an eighty-year-old man for swiping a few flowers.

"No, ma'am. It's stealing and I'm not proud of the fact."

Katherine turned to look at Dean, but couldn't make out his expression because of the darkness. He was directing the beam of the flashlight at her and Edison. He was allowing her to handle the situation. She wasn't sure if she was thankful or not. "Edison, can I ask you why you just didn't ask Ida for the flowers? She would have gladly given them to you."

"Ida and my beloved wife, Pauline, had a rivalry going for years on who grew the best flowers. Pauline had magical hands when it came to gardening. You should have seen our yard. Flowers in every conceivable color. They were so bright it hurt your eyes just to look at them." Edison's voice held a faraway tone, as if he were seeing the past.

Dean cleared his throat and said softly for Katherine's benefit. "Edison's wife passed away last summer."

Edison shuffled his feet on the brick walkway. "Having fresh flowers in the house brings back so many fond memories of her. I tried tending her gardens last year when she was so ill, but everything I touched died." He gave a watery chuckle. "Pauline always did swear I had a brown thumb."

Katherine felt the moisture in her eyes threaten to overflow. She couldn't imagine loving someone so much that after that person's death she would sneak around in the dead of night stealing flowers, just because they brought back sweet memories. She glanced at Dean's silhouette and the imagining became easier.

"Edison." She gently touched the elderly man's hands. "You may have as many of Ida's flowers as you want. Ida loves giving away her flowers. I'll see to it that she brings you fresh ones every couple of days." By the beam of the flashlight she could see the tears welling up in Edison's eyes. "We don't want you wandering around the gardens at night, because the pathways are uneven and you might get hurt."

"I would appreciate that, ma'am." Edison squeezed her fingers once before dropping her

Silver in the Moonlight
201

hand. "Now, if you would excuse me. I think I'll be heading back home."

"Wait, Edison, aren't you forgetting something." Katherine bent down and picked up the flowers he had already cut and the small pruning shears he had dropped in his fright. She handed him the flowers and cut a couple more snapdragons to add to the bouquet. "You better go put them in some water." She kissed his cheek. "Please be careful on your way home."

"Thank you, ma'am." Edison nodded to Dean and slowly made his way back out of the garden, clutching his flowers and using the flashlight as his guide.

Katherine watched him go with tears shimmering in her eyes. Dean wrapped an arm around her shoulders and pulled her close. "That's so sad, Dean."

He brushed a kiss across the top of her head. "You, Miss Katherine Rochelle Silver, have the biggest heart in all of South Carolina."

"I do not." She sniffled and blinked back the remaining tears. "Edison must have loved his wife very much."

"I'm sure he did." Dean tilted up her chin. "Now that you promised him fresh flowers from Ida's gardens, what are you going to do when the landscaper comes and rips most of this out? Ida's already agreed upon cutting back not only the number of gardens, but the size of them as well."

"I can get Edison fresh flowers anywhere.

There's a little florist in town. Heck, even the local Piggly Wiggly sells bunches of fresh flowers at the cash registers."

"Like I said, the biggest heart in all of South Carolina." He brushed another light kiss across her cheek. "Do you think there's still room in there for me?"

Her mouth moved instinctively toward his. "Room?" She chuckled as she teased the corner of his mouth. "When are you going to realize that you own the whole darn thing?"

He crushed her mouth beneath his. His low groan of desire vibrated in his chest as she wrapped her arms around his neck and pulled him closer. This was where she belonged, in Dean's arms.

She nearly cried out as he released her mouth and glanced around the moonlit garden. Before she could protest, he swung her up into his arms and carried her toward an iron bench tucked beneath a magnolia tree. He sat down and set her on his lap. "We need to talk, Kate."

She nibbled a path up the side of his neck to the sensitive spot directly behind his ear. She had learned from experience that kissing that particular spot could send him over the edge. "We'll talk later."

He shuddered and pushed her away as her lips found their mark. "Play fair, Kate." He held her shoulders so she couldn't kiss him again. "We need to talk about this afternoon."

Silver in the Moonlight

"I don't want to talk." She pulled his head closer. "I love you, Dean Warren Katz."

At her words of love, Dean abandoned all restraint and gave her the kind of kiss that was guaranteed to curl her toes permanently. She melted into his embrace.

"Oh my!" cried Ida.

"Goodness me!" exclaimed Sadie.

If it hadn't been for Dean's arms, Katherine would have fallen off his lap. She jerked her head around and stared at her aunts. Both were wearing their nightgowns and ankle-length light-colored robes. They looked like a pair of specters haunting the garden.

Sadie's hair was up in sponge curlers and she was holding a wicked-looking rolling pin. Ida was clutching the lapels on her robe so tight, her knuckles were whiter than her hair and a brass candlestick was trembling in her other hand. She appeared thoroughly shocked, while Sadie looked only startled. But both appeared ready to confront the flower thief on their own.

It was a real shame they hadn't been there twenty minutes earlier, Katherine thought. She shook her head at her aunts. "You're too late."

"Oh my," Ida said, clearly getting the wrong idea of the situation.

"Not for that, Ida," Katherine said quickly. "We already caught the flower thief and sent him home."

"You did?" Ida asked.

"Who was it?" Sadie asked.

"Edison Burleigh from up the street. It seems fresh flowers in the house remind him of Pauline and he was afraid to ask Ida for some since there was some type of argument between her and his late wife about who grew the best flowers." She refused to be embarrassed because she'd been caught necking with Dean, again. Her aunts would just have to get used to the idea that she was going to kiss Dean anytime or anyplace she liked.

"Oh my," moaned Ida.

"I hope you told him he could have as many as he likes." Sadie shook her head. "Poor Edison, he was so devoted to Pauline."

"I told him Ida would be more than glad to supply him with fresh flowers anytime she had some in bloom. You don't mind, do you, Ida?"

"Of course not. Pauline was a wonderful gardener. I don't know why I haven't thought of bringing him flowers sooner." Ida placed the candlestick in the large pocket of her robe and glared at Dean. "What do you have to say for yourself now, young man?"

Katherine groaned and dropped her forehead against Dean's chest. Her dear, sweet, interfering aunt was once again asking the man his intentions.

"I'm sorry, Ida, but I will not be marrying Kate just because you caught us kissing for the second time today."

Silver in the Moonlight
205

Katherine raised her head and stared at him in horror. Here she had been planning to accept his hasty proposal and now he was taking it back.

He glanced down at her and smiled. "I'm going to marry her because I love her and she loves me."

The sound of delight that sprang from her throat startled a couple of sleeping birds in the magnolia tree above them. She wrapped her arms around his neck and smothered his face with quick little kisses.

"Oh my!" Ida said.

"Hush, Ida," Sadie scolded. "Can't you see they want to be alone?"

"But we can't leave them alone. It's improper."

"Maybe if Pa had left us alone with some of our beaux, we wouldn't be the old spinsters we are today. Leave them be. Dean said he was going to marry her. What more do you want?"

Ida's voice faded as they walked back to the house. "I guess it will be all right for a few minutes."

Katherine continued to kiss Dean, only half listening to her aunts. She had to smile against Dean's throat when she heard Sadie ask Ida if she thought Edison Burleigh might like cherry pie. Between her aunts, the poor man wouldn't know what hit him.

Dean captured her face in his hands. "Am I

right in assuming this is an affirmative answer to my clumsily asked question from this afternoon?"

"Try getting out of it, buster, and I'll sic my aunts on you. Lord knows Ida already thinks you've compromised me." She teased the corner of his mouth with the tip of her tongue.

He retaliated by nipping at her lower lip. "Have I compromised you, sweet Kate?"

"Indubitably. You've ruined me for every other man."

"Good," he growled as he captured her mouth once again.

She was being pulled under the tide of his kisses when her aunt's voice penetrated the haze of desire.

"Kitty," Sadie called through the thick overgrown gardens. "Do you know what I just thought of?"

Katherine reluctantly broke the kiss and pouted. "What did you just think of, Aunt Sadie?"

"Once you marry Dean, your name is going to be Kitty Katz." Sadie's laugh could be heard until she entered the house and the screen door closed behind her.

She glanced at Dean, who was valiantly trying to hold back his own laughter. "One word, Dean, and I'll make you change your last name before I marry you." Oh, Lord, why hadn't she thought of that before? Kitty Katz! It made her sound like some exotic dancer!

Dean pressed a finger against his mouth. "My lips are sealed, Kate."

She leaned forward and pressed her mouth to his. "Seal it with a kiss."

He pulled her closer and lightly ran his tongue over her lips. "I'll seal it with anything you want, love, as long as you become my wife and I can kiss you anywhere and anytime I want without Ida looking at me as if I'm committing a sin."

She ran her fingers up his arm, over his broad shoulders. Her mouth found the sensitive spot behind his ear. "Well, if it's sin you want to be committing . . ."

EPILOGUE

Dean pulled his new wife into his arms and started to wake her with his mouth. Over the past several weeks he had learned a great deal about Katherine Rochelle Silver Katz. One, she didn't like to be awakened without a cup of coffee beneath her nose. And two, which was more important to his way of thinking, Kate loved making love when the morning sun was just starting to streak in through the windows. This morning his timing was perfect.

He wanted this morning to be special. It was their first morning together in their own bed, in their own home. Kate had scandalized her aunts by insisting that not only would their wedding take place the last Saturday in June, but it would to be held in Jasper instead of Boston. Practically the entire town had been invited and had shown up for the wedding.

Silver in the Moonlight

Kate had also insisted that Dean take her to Charleston so she could meet his parents, sister, and grandfather. He had thought the trip would be a disaster, but instead it had turned out all right. His father had offered him an olive branch and seemed immensely proud of the fact that Dean was starting his own banking empire without the backing of the Katz's fortune. His whole family had come to Jasper for the wedding.

Kate's family was the bigger surprise. Not only had her father crossed the Mason-Dixon Line to attend the wedding and give away the bride, he had also made peace with Sadie and Ida. He had even gone so far as to offer his aunts a place to stay while the majority of the construction was being done on their home. The day after Kate and Dean left for their honeymoon, Edward had escorted his aunts to Boston.

On the way home from Hawaii they had stopped in Boston for a few days. Sadie and Ida were in their glory, bustling around the kitchen and the gardens as if they'd lived there for years. Kate's parents and brother all appeared to have gained a little weight since the wedding. It had been a joyous sight.

Dean pulled his thoughts away from Kate's family and watched as the first blush of dawn splashed across their bed and lightened his wife's nipples to a dusty pink. He placed a kiss on each tip and grinned with delight as they perked into tight little berries.

Kate arched her back and glared at the light filtering through the lace curtains. "Is it morning already?"

He chuckled against her stomach. "Good morning, Mrs. Katz." His tongue circled her navel and dipped inside for a quick taste.

She wiggled beneath him and trailed a hand up the outside of his thigh. "Good morning, yourself, Mr. Katz." Her hand wrapped around his arousal. "My, my, aren't you up bright and early."

He thrust himself into her hand and groaned. The little witch knew exactly what to do to him to bring him to the edge. Who would have thought he would have made love to her in Ida's garden the night she accepted his proposal? He didn't even want to think about the night in Hawaii when they'd ended up swimming naked in the ocean. He had been very glad that no one had been strolling the beach at two A.M. "Kate, sweetheart, I love you dearly, but we have to slow down."

She pulled him closer and strung kisses up his neck to the spot behind his ear. "Why?"

"I want this to be special." He groaned as she wrapped her legs around his waist and smiled that special smile that made him feel like a god. "It's our first morning waking up together in our home."

"Dean, when are you going to learn that every time we make love is special?" The tips of her breasts brushed his chest.

He couldn't control it any longer. He had to have her, now, this instant. With one forceful thrust he entered her and completed their union. After brushing a kiss across her mouth, he raised his head and looked down at her radiant face. "Is it any wonder that I love you so much?"

She pulled his head back down to hers and tightened her legs around his waist. "You're only saying that because Sadie gave me the recipe for her chocolate-chip cookies."

THE EDITORS' CORNER

With Halloween almost over, Thanksgiving and Christmas are not far behind, and we hope the following four books will be at the top of your shopping list. It's not often that you can find everything you need in one store! All these sexy heroes have a special talent, whether it's rubbing the tension from a woman's shoulders or playing the bagpipes. You may just want to keep these guys around the house!

Cheryln Biggs presents **THIEF OF MIDNIGHT**, LOVESWEPT #910. When Clanci James stepped into the smoky bar, she'd already resigned herself to what she was about to do—find sexy Jake Walker, seduce him, drug him, and kidnap him. The creep was the one sabotaging her ranch, her grandfather was sure of it. So, while he looked for clues to incriminate Jake, Clanci had to keep him out of the way. When Jake comes to, he's alone, got a heck of a hangover, and he's tied to Clanci's bed. Insisting he's not the one who's kidnapped her horse, he promises to help a suspicious Clanci. As the search for the missing horse continues, Clanci and Jake are confined to close quarters, a situation that quickly reveals their real feelings. Clanci's been through love turned bad . . . will she throw caution out the window to chance love again? Cheryln Biggs throws a feisty cowgirl together with the rugged rancher next door.

A **FIRST-CLASS MALE** is hard to find, but in LOVESWEPT #911 Donna Valentino introduces Connor Hughes to one Shelby Ferguson, a woman in need of a good man. Connor is faced with two hundred hungry people and a miserable tuna casserole big enough to feed maybe fifty, at one noodle apiece. Apparently it *is* his problem when people show up to a potluck dinner without the potluck. So, when Shelby arrives with the catering vans, Connor knows his guardian angel is working overtime. Shelby's sister just got dumped at the altar, and there's enough food to feed, well, a hungry potluck crowd. Scared of the Ferguson curse that's haunted her all her life, Shelby won't risk her heart for anything but a sure thing. And if that means a staid but secure man, then so be it. But nowhere does it say she *has* to help out this seemingly unreliable guy. Never one to desert a person in need, Shelby offers to help Connor out in restoring Miss Stonesipher's house. Donna Valentino charts a splendidly chaotic course that will lead to a terrifically happy ending.

Jill Shalvis gives us the poignant **LEAN ON ME**, LOVESWEPT #912. Desperate to escape her old life, Clarissa Woods walked into The Right Place knowing that the clinic would be her salvation. Little did she know that its owner, Bo Tyler, would be as well. Bo has his own battles to fight, and fight he does, every day of his life. But his hope is renewed when he sets eyes on Clarissa. No one had ever treated Clarissa with kindness and compassion, but when she returns it, he still has his doubts. Together they work toward making his clinic a success, but will they take time to explore their special kinship? Jill Shalvis celebrates the heart's astonishing capacity for healing when she places one life in the hands—and heart—of its soul mate.

Kathy Lynn Emerson wows us once again in **THAT SPECIAL SMILE**, LOVESWEPT #913. Russ didn't know when his daughter had chosen to grow up, but he was definitely going to kill the woman who'd convinced her to enter the Special Smile contest. When he realizes that Tory Grenville is none other than Vicki MacDougall from high school, he coerces her to chaperon Amanda in the pageant. Tory doesn't really know anything about being in beauty pageants. At Amanda's age, she hadn't yet grown into her body, or gained the confidence only adulthood can give. But Russ is determined, and a guilty Tory can't very well say no. She teams up with Russ to get Amanda through the pageant, but when he starts to take an interest in her as a woman, Tory knows she's in trouble. Russ the school jock was one thing, but Russ the handsome heartthrob is another. Kathy Lynn Emerson offers the irresistible promise that maybe a few high school dreams can come true.

Happy reading!

With warmest wishes,

Susann Brailey   Joy Abella

Susann Brailey   Joy Abella
Senior Editor   Administrative Editor